CAMERON

N.J. ADEL

This is a work of fiction. All incidents and dialogue, and all characters are products of the author's imagination. Any resemblance to persons living or dead, similar books or characters is entirely coincidental.

Copyright © 2022 N.J. Adel
All rights reserved.
ISBN: 9798355473723
Salacious Queen Publishing

DEDICATION

To women who can bring alpha holes to their
knees
It's time someone taught those motherfuckers
a lesson

ALSO BY N.J. ADEL

Contemporary Romance
The Italian Heartthrob
The Italian Happy Ever After
The Italian Marriage
The Italian Obsession
The Italian Dom
The Italian Son

Paranormal Reverse Harem
All the Teacher's Pet Beasts
All the Teacher's Little Belles
All the Teacher's Bad Boys
All the Teacher's Prisoners

Reverse Harem Erotic Romance
Her Royal Harem: Complete Box Set

Dark MC and Mafia Romance
Furore
Tirone
Dusty
Cameron
Night Skulls Mayhem

TABLE OF CONTENTS

CHAPTER 1

DUSTY

The second Cammie walked out of the door, a switch in me flipped. Watching the only woman I loved slip away from me wasn't an option.

I knew she never belonged to my world. My father hurt her and her family beyond repair. I didn't make things better. I scared her, and I'd hurt her with my words and actions. I should let her go to live the life she deserved, not the one I was dragging her down to. But all that meant nothing to me the moment she vanished behind that door.

Cammie was mine. I was no fucking righteous hero or saint to let her go. If that made me the villain, so be it. *I'd never let her go.*

Blood still staining my hands, I dashed after her. "Cammie!"

She faltered down the hall, clutching the strap of her bag, but then she didn't stop. She sped toward the elevator.

I ran, blocking her way. "I can't let you leave like that."

She wouldn't even look at me. "Dusty, please. I've made up my mind. Don't make this harder than it already is."

A lump clogged my throat. "At least…let me take you home."

"I can take care of myself."

"It's late, and with you dressed like that…" She was a fucking knockout, and my blood had been simmering all night because of the way fuckers like that piece of shit Samuel were looking at her even when I was with her. I almost killed that asshole for it. It was what got us in this shit in the first place.

"You don't have to worry about me. Like I said, I can take care of myself, and I'm no longer your—"

"No longer what? You'll always be mine, Cammie." If any prick so much as breathed on her wrong when I wasn't with her, it wouldn't be a few punches I'd throw. I didn't care about her approval or how much of a monster she'd think I'd become, but if there was anyone I'd kill for again and again without a second thought, it was Cammie.

"Dusty—"

"Please, for my sanity. Let me drive you home. It's not too much to ask."

Her jaws clenched as she studied the hotel floor carpet. Her not looking at me drove me nuts. She couldn't have hated me this much not to be able to bring herself to look at me.

"If I say yes, will you promise to leave and go back to Rosewood and never come back?"

How could she fucking ask me that? I'd never make that promise, and she knew it. I gritted all the words and curses jumping to my tongue under my teeth. She wouldn't accept any apology, explanation, promise or groveling right now. "Let me take you home safe, Cameron." I wasn't asking.

She sighed, and I was ready to drag her and put her on my bike until we reached her apartment whether she liked it or not if she said no. Fuck, I was ready to lie to her, to kidnap her all the way to Rosewood, tie her to my bed and never let her out. There was no fucking way in hell I'd let her break up with me. She was mine.

I was hers.

She gave me a terse nod. She must have read my tone or sensed the blaze of heat bubbling up under my skin and decided to stop fighting me. My ol'lady knew me better than my own Mama.

In the elevator, I couldn't take my eyes off her, while her bloodshot eyes were pinned to her shoes, our heated breaths replacing the heavy words swarming in our chests.

When we reached the parking lot, I took off my jacket and put it on her shoulders. It'd be cold for her in that dress on the bike. When she flinched, I was about to snap. "Stop doing that. You know I'll never ever fucking hurt you. And for fuck's sake, look at me."

Her lips twitched, and her head barely lifted, as she shrugged into my jacket and circled herself with her arms.

"Please, baby," I whispered.

A tear dropped down her face, and I couldn't just stand there. Without thinking, I pulled her into my embrace. My arms wrapped tight around her, and she shook against my body, her tears soaking my shirt.

My heart ached with every whimper, but a flicker of hope pulsed within me. Now that she wasn't afraid to be in my arms, maybe there was a chance she wouldn't leave me. I printed little kisses on top of her head, filling my nostrils with her scent, gluing my arms around her body. She cried harder, and I wished I could have taken it all away, what happened tonight, the pain I caused her, the past, everything. "I'm sorry. Please forgive me. Don't leave me. I'd do anything, sweetheart."

She sniffled, pulling away, and the hope I thought I had faded. I stalled, but she wriggled out of my embrace and wiped her face. "I just wanna go home."

She marched toward my bike before I could say anything. I followed her as thunder broke the sky, echoing the sound of my heart. As we cruised down the road, rain whipped at me, but I wasn't cold. Not when my Cammie was sitting behind me, her body on my back, and her warmth surrounded me.

Warmth she'd take away from me for God knew how long.

I sped, my heart hollowing with the cold void of missing her already. I couldn't live with that. There had to be something I could do to make her stay.

"Wait… This isn't the way back to my place," she said.

My eyes squinted at the open road as I accelerated more.

Her body tensed against mine as we had the road to ourselves. "Dusty! Where the fuck are you taking me?!"

"Relax. I'm not gonna kidnap you." I'd thought about it. Honestly, the only thing stopping me was her school. She worked so hard to get back to it. If I ruined it for her, she'd never forgive me.

"Then where are you going?!"

I slowed down, and then I pulled over by the roadside, dark rain pouring on us. She hopped off the bike in a flash. "Are you gonna tell me what the fuck you're doing?"

My gaze locked on hers, taking in that beauty that had brought me to my knees from the moment we met, that was now, while she wore my clothes, her makeup and hair a mess under the rain, seemed to have increased tenfold. "I'm gonna put my life in your hands."

She shook her head. "What?"

"I'm breaking all the rules, Cammie. I will show you that nothing matters to me more than you."

"Dusty, what are you talking about? What are you gonna do?"

CHAPTER 2

DUSTY

"I can't ride your bike," Cameron said incredulously.

"As the president of the Night Skulls, I say you can." Even if no rules allowed ol'ladies to do so.

"Why? I'm not your ol'lady anymore."

My fist clenched. "Can you stop saying that? I'm not breaking up with you, Cammie."

"But I am. There's nothing that's going to change—"

Whatever she was saying turned into a yelp when I carried her over my shoulder caveman style and put her back on my bike.

She squirmed. "What the fuck?"

I held her still, not giving her any freedom or space to hop off again. Then I stared at her big brown eyes that were wet and mascara smeared. "You're the only woman who has brought me to my knees. I respect you, and I submit to you lovingly and willingly, but when it comes to losing you, there isn't an ounce of me that will submit. There's nothing I wouldn't do to change your mind and win you back, Cammie. Even if it means *I* will have to bring *you* to your knees."

Her jaw dropped. "What's that supposed to mean?"

"It means tonight, I'll tell you what to do, and you will obey like a good girl."

I could hear the snort coming out of her throat, but before she had a chance to let it out, I climbed behind her, pushing her with my size to the front and held her hands.

"Dusty, stop. You can't—"

The feeling of my cock pushing into her ass as I pushed my hips, spreading my legs silenced her. The little gasp that escaped her satisfied me; she still fucking wanted me. Bringing her hands to the handlebars, I leaned in, licking the rain drops off her neck. Then I whispered, "What did I just say?" I bit her earlobe, her sweet shivers to my touch running through me. "Be a good a girl and drive."

"You know very goddamn well I'm not a good girl."

I bit her neck with a rough, hungry kiss. "Then I'll teach you how to be *my* good girl."

She scoffed. "I'm not driving, Dusty. You can't force me."

I bit harder, and pinched her nipple over her dress. "Try me."

She moaned a swear and a threat, her hand reaching to remove mine now cupping her tit, but I started the bike for her, using my feet, my weight crushing her, rendering her immobile.

"What the fuck?!" she yelled as the engine revved, and the bike jerked in motion.

"If you don't take over now, we'll crash." I removed my hand off the bar.

As the bike swayed, threatening to veer off the road, she gripped the bar with both her hands, getting it under control before we licked the asphalt. "You're crazy!"

I pushed harder into the flesh of her ass, a hard-on aching inside my pants. "Crazy for you, sweetheart."

Her heart raced against my hand, and her tits rose and fell fast. "This is… ridiculous. What about the dress I'm wearing? At least, behind you, no one could see my underwear. Now, I'm on fucking display."

"You think I haven't thought about this? I'll be damned before I put you on display for any fucker to see your beauty. You're mine, baby." This road was the shortcut I took back to Rosewood. At this time of the night, no one was usually on that road for miles. "We have the road to ourselves, but just to be sure…" I slid my other hand down her body and reached between her thighs.

"Nononono, No. You can't—"

I stifled her words for the millionth time tonight when I pushed down the edge of her panties and cupped her pussy bare. She trembled with a gasp that sent my dick digging a hole in my pants. I parted her lips and circled her clit before I entered my middle finger in her sweet wetness.

Her hair swung behind her back and tickled my face as she tilted her head back. "Oh my God. OH MY GOD!"

I let another finger in and thrust in and out while my thumb moved on her now swollen clit, enjoying how wet she became by the second. "Eyes on the road, sweetheart. If you close them, we die."

"Sh-shit."

I upped the pace, squeezing her tit at the same time. "I trust you."

"You can't do this."

"I can, and I'm doing it. My life is in your hands, baby. I trust you with it." I hoped with that she could regain her trust in me, too. I hoped she'd understand I loved her more than anything, I'd never hurt her, and I was ready to do anything for her. "Even if we crashed, I'd die a happy man, knowing I was touching you, giving you the pleasure you deserve."

"I-I... Oh God."

"No, baby. Dusty. There's no god here. Only me and you." I fucked her with my fingers, and she rode them, chasing the orgasm I was about to give her. "And if anyone is worth worshiping, it's you, my goddess. I'm yours."

Her heart rocketed, and her chest heaved. She rubbed against me fast, her gorgeous lips wide gasping for air. I knew she was so close, dripping all over my palm.

"Dusty," she gasped, "I'm...ahh..."

"I know, baby. I know." I pulled out my fingers just before she came. "But not just yet."

"What the fuck?!" Her hair whipped as she glared at me. "You fucking shitting me?"

I smirked. "Do you need me?"

"Fuck you."

"Say it, Cammie. Tell me you need me."

"You're such an asshole."

"An asshole that can't fucking live without you. Tell me you're mine, Cammie. Say it."

She pulled over and jerked out of my grasp. Then she swung her leg to get off the bike. I dismounted it before her and held her still. "Where the fuck do you think you're going?"

"We broke up, Dusty. I shouldn't have come with you. This is a mistake."

Fury surged in me. "A mistake?"

She tried to leave. "You gotta let me go."

I pinned her down, pushing her a little so she'd lie back on the bike. Then I hopped back on, spreading her legs and then hooking them behind my back. "Never."

"Dusty, what are you doing?"

I unzipped my pants. "Showing you who you really belong to."

Her eyes widened, and she looked around at the dark emptiness. "No. Enough. This isn't going to bring us back together. It's over."

I tore her fucking panties and hiked her dress up. Her pussy glistened at me, pink and ripe, and my cock jerked. "I didn't hear you complaining when you were about to drench my hand a minute ago."

"Dusty, I'm serious." Her breath hitched. "Let me go."

I pushed inside her. How wet she was swelled my balls, driving me feral. "If you don't want this," I thrust deeper, my Prince Albert hitting her clit, "if you don't need me," I groaned with another thrust as her pussy swallowed whole my Jacob's Ladder, "tell me to stop."

CHAPTER 3

CAMERON

Breathing was a task I seemed to forget how to perform when he filled me like that, let alone speaking.

I was heartbroken, furious and devastated, but my whole being was reduced to the feeling of him inside me, blowing my mind as if it was the first time he fucked me into oblivion.

With every thrust, every ecstatic sensation rippling inside me, my mind turned into a black void incapable of weighing danger or using logic. Nothing there but the waves of pleasure, spreading to every nerve, forcing me, for once, into sweet, dangerous submission.

He fucked me harder on his bike, on the street, in the middle of nowhere. Dirty. Depraved. And so fucking hot. "That's right. You take me, baby. Take all of me like a good girl. *My* good girl."

"Fuck!" I screamed like a whore as he drove me over to the edge.

"Good girl. Scream for me." His prompts and the way he hammered into me dragged even louder screams out of my throat. "Let the whole world know who owns your pretty little pussy."

I'd never felt Dusty's dominant side at full capacity. I'd never imagined he could have been that carnal and possessive when he took over. I'd never thought I'd have enjoyed it this much, not when I loved being on top, and especially not after I saw how deadly carnal and possessive he could be in life itself and not just in sex.

It turned out my body didn't give a shit. My pussy worshipped him as much as he worshipped me. Nothing mattered when his big, pierced cock was filling and stretching me.

This is wrong. This is so fucking wrong. I pushed into him, letting him in deeper with no shame, until I exploded around him. Then it wasn't only my cum flooding me. His warm, thick seed spurted inside me.

"Fuck, baby." The rain had stopped, but his shirt was wet, strained over his huge muscles, his hair dripping on his sated chiseled face. He looked like a god sent on a mission to fuck this one moral—me. "How could you ever ask me to walk away from this, from you?"

"We have to stop," I panted. "This isn't right."

"No, baby. I can't stop. I ain't done with you yet." He smirked, not pulling out, surprisingly still hard. "When I'm done with you, you're gonna feel me for days."

The haze of pleasure swallowed me again, and I convinced myself every couple should have one more session of mind blowing sex at breakup. Things didn't have to be ugly—even when they were viciously ugly. Of course, that was my pussy talking.

Dusty's fingers and eyes were on my inner thigh, and then I felt him lap the little cum that spilled on my skin and push it back inside me. A faint sound whispered from a distance in my head. Then a sudden horror attacked me. "Fuck. No. Dusty…what the fuck are you doing?"

"Putting it back where it belonged."

"You're gonna get me pregnant. I'm not on birth control."

"I know."

"Dusty, are you crazy? Are you doing this on purpose?"

He pushed inside me faster, harder, hungrier, as if putting a baby inside me turned him on so vigorously. "I always came inside you, baby. It never bothered you before."

I swallowed. "Before, we were together." It wasn't like we made love every day. I saw him once a week, and I took one of those pills the morning after. Even if anything had happened, we could have figured it out together. "Now, we're not."

His smirk vanished, replaced by the wild rage that had been popping in his eyes all night. "Stop fucking saying that. You're mine." He slammed into me, proving a point. "Say it, Cameron. Whose pussy is this?"

I moaned idiotically, thinking with my ovaries, but I managed to shake my head.

He fisted my hair, his hips undulating, as he pulled my legs up a little for a better penetration angle. "Fine. I'm gonna keep filling you up until you say it."

"Fuck, Dusty. No."

"Yes." His hips crushed mine. "Fucking yes. A million times yes." He made me take his thick ropes of cum as he pushed my ankles back to my shoulders, determined to give me every drop and keep it inside.

Our gazes locked, and our labored breaths danced the dance of war. I should be raging and fighting, but the part of me—perhaps all of me—that loved Dusty understood where his actions came from. He loved and wanted me more than anything, and so did I. I might have even found what he'd just done to me hot, and my heart was begging me to forgive his violent tendencies and stay.

I wished I could have.

His face paled, as if he could read my eyes and what I wanted to say without words. "Cammie, no. I love you."

A tear fled my eye as the images of Samuel's smashed, bloody face haunted me. "I love you, too," I rasped, but I knew if I didn't leave now, I wouldn't pull Dusty out of the Night Skulls like he thought he could so we'd live together in peace. It was I that was going to be a Night Skull, living by their hideous code of sickness, evil, murder and mayhem, betraying my sister's memory, turning into a monster like the ones who raped and murdered her. "I can't. I'm sorry."

His bright eyes dimmed and misted. "Cammie…"

I held his face between my hands and crushed my lips on his. One last time.

CHAPTER 4

DUSTY

She just needs space.

I kept telling myself that as I thundered into the night back to Rosewood. The humid, cold air lay heavy on my face and lungs as I reached South Beach. The bay looked dead on this moonless night and the hills deader.

The salty wind retracted as I rode farther through the hills. I rounded an unmarked turn that led straight to a dirt road flanked by untamed greenery. The hidden path to what was supposed to be *home*. Except that Rosewood never felt like home for me. Ever.

I only knew the meaning of that word in Cameron's arms.

I'm an idiot. I shouldn't have let her leave. Should've stopped her. Kidnapped her like she thought I was.

Shit. What the fuck is happening to me?

Maybe she was right. The club was really messing with my head or worse. Maybe I was my father's son after all.

No! I kicked the thought out of my head. The bright lights and rock music from the estate greeted me as I killed the engine of my Harley.

It was after three a.m., and the party was still going. A bonfire in the front yard. Hammered brothers in beach chairs barely lifting their hands to wave at me. Fucking sounds came from inside the house as I climbed the patio stairs. 'Hey, Prez' low murmurs accompanied me as I walked through spilled beer, side-stepped naked bodies strewn all around, and turned down the stereo behind the bar.

"All right. Party is over, Skulls," I commanded, grabbing a bottle of tequila from the liquor cabinet.

The slightly-sober brothers started to ease out of the living room and the halls. The others would be dead till the afternoon. I wouldn't bother wake them.

I grabbed a glass and downed a shot. Then I decided to take the bottle to my room. If I walked into Mama or that fucker Rush now, I'd wage another war. My rage had caused me a lot tonight. Damage that I didn't know how to fix. Whether it could be fixed. Enough damage for one night.

I dragged myself and the tequila upstairs to my room, men and women still spilling out to their own rooms or outside where they would continue the party somewhere else.

Rosewood was a huge estate. Roar had got it in exchange for some ass gambler's debt and life. A mansion of sorts with plenty of room for the Skulls and their fucktoys. Secluded and swallowed by a small forest. Perfect for the club and business. It was pretty before, but now it was a dump. The pool drained. The garden a disaster. Even the paint and wallpaper inside washed out.

Finally, I reached my *chambers*. The only clean place here. Nobody ever bothered to clean in Rosewood, and if I hadn't told them to keep my room nice, it would have been a dump, too.

I locked the door and plopped down on the bed. Then I downed three more shots in quick succession. The look Cameron gave me before she left wouldn't quit haunting me.

With the patch on my back and the tattoos spread on my body, people always had looked at me as a Night Skull, assuming the worst, whether I'd done it or not.

Sure, I'd broken laws. A fucking lot of them. But I wasn't a rapist. Or a murderer per se. I'd never taken a life before Roar's, not even by accident or order. He was the only soul I'd taken, and it was to save the girl that I loved.

That didn't stop everyone from thinking I was a ruthless thug capable of all the dark shit anyone could imagine. But not my Cammie. She always looked at me without the fear in everybody else's eyes. Even in the bunker. She saw me. Dustin not Dusty.

I never wanted to lose that. Now, it was all gone. It didn't matter that I was defending her. She still looked at me like I was the monster she dreaded.

She trusted me, and I betrayed that trust. If I could beat a man like that in front of her, what would I do when I was away? The shit I'd said didn't help either. *You know as much as I do some fuckers deserve to die. It's a necessity.* What the fuck was I thinking?

Maybe I should've told her I'd never killed after Roar, not in the stupid fucking way I blamed her for it. That didn't fucking help at all. She had every right to think I was a fucking murderer that did it whenever I felt like it.

If I was being honest, if she hadn't stopped me, I had no problem killing that piece of shit that tried to grope her. Maybe her fears weren't for nothing. The bylaws I lived by, the power that grew on me, the longer I stayed in the club deemed murder an inevitable crime I was bound to commit sooner or later.

I closed my eyes, feeling the burn of the unshed tears, cursing myself to hell and beyond. Then I had another shot. I got off the bed, threw the glass and drank directly from the bottle. As I staggered in the room, I came across my reflection in the dresser mirror, and for a second I saw what she saw.

The sickening anger. The wasted expression. The evil lurking underneath. Even though we never had the same features, I did look like Roar now.

I hurled the bottle at the mirror, smashing both in pieces. Then I ran through the woods, screaming at the invisible moon in a drunken rage until I passed out.

CHAPTER 5

CAMERON

I spent the weekend, and the couple after, wallowing in my room, blaming myself for everything that had happened, questioning my decision over and over.

The events of that bloody Valentine played in my head like a broken record. I couldn't help wondering if there was something I could have said or done for the night to have taken a different course.

One that would let me be with the only man I loved and missed so fucking much.

Had I overreacted? Was I wrong about letting Dusty go? Was he really just protecting me and Samuel did deserve it?

Ash, despite being Dusty's number one fan, was unexpectedly on my side. "A punch or two would've sufficed, but that was crazy," she'd said. Ashley had become my voice of sanity when missing him messed with my conscience, assuring me I did the right thing.

But why did doing the right thing hurt so goddamn much?

She'd tried everything to drag me out of the apartment. A movie. A drink. A party. But I kept telling her I had to study. Even if I wasn't that devastated about the breakup, how would I face the people from school if I ran into any of them? I saw how Samuel's friends looked at Dusty and me as we ran off like criminals before the cops arrived.

God only knew what Dusty had told Samuel so he wouldn't press charges, but I was certain it was menacing enough. From what I heard, the douche didn't utter a word.

Eventually, Ash gave up on getting me out of my room, and I hadn't opened a book. I'd switched off my phone, too, and gave it to her. Crazy, right? But I had to. I knew if I heard Dusty's voice I'd break. And I knew he would call. A lot.

I turned on the TV in the living room, begging for anything boring to help me doze off, but I wasn't really watching. The nights were the worst. I couldn't sleep. Even when my body would give in, the nightmares hit. More vicious than before.

A key rattle made me look over my shoulder. The door opened, and Ash popped in. "All right, look what I've smuggled from the frat house all the way here?" She hopped over the couch, giggling, and revealed a bottle of vodka tucked under her jacket.

"We're stealing booze now?"

"And weed." She nodded, her eyes glazed, and reached inside her pocket, bringing out a couple of fat joints. "You won't go to the party, so I bring it to you here." She got a lighter from her jeans pocket, lit one of the joints, and handed it to me. "Here."

I didn't mind anything that might knock me out, so I took a drag. "You didn't have to leave the party on my account. I'm fine."

"Totally didn't." She took the joint between the tips of her thumb and index finger. "It was lame anyway."

That was a lie. In the past couple of days, she never stayed out late or left the apartment after I fell asleep. A true friend that I loved so much, and with her petite self, she reminded me a lot of my sister.

My arms flung around her, holding her tight. She hugged me back with equal care. "Thank you, Ash." I broke our embrace to look at her, tears burning around the corners of my eyes. "For everything."

A warm smile lit her face. Then she shook the vodka bottle in my face. "We doing this or what?"

"Sure." I sniffled. "I have a feeling we'll be doing this every night from now on. Hangovers are good excuses to skip class in the morning."

"Oh c'mon," she said as I fetched two glasses from the kitchenette attached to the living room. "You can't hide here forever."

"Can't I?" I sank in the couch, placing the glasses on the coffee table.

"Not if you wanna get your degree." She blew a big puff of the joint and handed it to me. Then she opened the bottle and poured our shots. "You worked so hard to get back to school. You can't throw that away because you think some dicks will look at you funny for being involved with the wrong boyfriend."

Wrong. No better way to describe it. Being with Dusty was wrong from the start. Wrong and twisted and sick.

Who could find love in such dark places where we'd been trapped? How could I've fallen for him so hard knowing exactly who he was? How could I've fallen at all after what had happened to my sister? How could he after what I'd done to him?

But we did, and it felt so fucking good. Not wrong at all. Perfect. Everything that had been traumatizing me since Annie's abduction, all the pain, the sadness, the heartache I couldn't shake on my own, melted under Dusty's scorching touch. He burned it all away, replacing it with everything I'd ever been searching for my whole life.

Love.

Trust.

A lump blocked my throat that I pushed down with the vodka, the weed already kicking in. "I know we didn't look like the right fit, but he was… Everything was going so well. He was going to leave and stay here with me…" Tears streamed down my face, hushing me.

"Cameron, you gotta focus on your future, girl. You're going to be an engineer. A great one. And you'll have your own harem of sexy big man candies that aren't on a killing spree."

I couldn't laugh. Actually, I got upset. I didn't want a harem of anything. Wrong or not, I wanted Dusty. The idea of being with someone else was…beyond my imagination.

"Do you think…?" I bit my lip in pain as I imagined him thinking about being with someone else. Rosewood must have been swarming with sluts throwing themselves at him now.

"Cameron!"

Ashley's yelp and the sound of glass breaking made me flinch. I glanced at her and then at my hand where she was staring. Fuck. I broke a glass absentmindedly just at the possibility of him with another woman. "Shit."

"I'll get you a towel and the first-aid kit." She jumped off the couch. "You think we should go to the ER?"

"No. I'll be fine." I gazed at the blood and shattered glass in my palm. I took some of the pieces out of my skin and poured some vodka on the wounds. It seared my flesh, but I wished it'd hurt ten times harder to mask the fire blazing inside me.

CHAPTER 6

DUSTY

The afternoon sun penetrating the tall trees and falling on my face woke me up. I squinted at it as I sat straight. My fingers ran through my hair, and dirt and dry leaves fell off. Great, I'd slept in the woods.

Standing, I dusted my jeans, and then I fished out my phone out of it. A few missed call alerts and text notifications were stuck on the screen but none from Cammie. Of course.

Without thinking, I called her. My heart banged as I anxiously waited to hear her voice, my feet crunching the twigs back to the house, the annoying dial tone ringing in my ear.

"Not here. Leave a message or call back later," her voicemail answered.

I knew she wouldn't pick up, but I needed to hear her voice, even if it was in that stupid message.

I called again. This time I spoke after the beep. "Just making sure you're all right. Please just let me know." I reached the front yard. A few brothers scattered around in the party aftermath, and Mama was standing on the porch, her eyes narrowed my way. "I love you, Cameron." My thumb tapped the red icon as Mama marched toward me.

She rubbed my arms, raking me from head to toe. "What the hell happened to you? When did you come back?"

"Last night."

"Did you spend the night out in the woods?" she asked in disbelief.

I glared at her, anger hitting again. I wouldn't forget she and my *trustworthy* VP contributed to last night's disaster. "Where's Rush?"

"What the fuck? Why did you sleep outside? And didn't you say you'd return on Monday? What the hell is going on?"

"She broke up with me. That's what's going on. Happy?" My chest heaved with heat and pain. "Now where the fuck is Rush?!"

She looked around, and I noticed the heads turning at our exchange. "Let's take this inside."

I beat her to my room, and she followed at her own pace. Kicking off my boots and tossing my cut on the bed, I could see the twitching, victorious smirk on her lips she didn't bother to hide.

"Before you give Rush a hard time, you gotta know he didn't tell me anything," she said once she closed the door. "I figured it out on my own."

"Where the fuck is he?" I asked slowly, closing my eyes in a failing attempt to control my temper.

"Sacramento to take care of the upcoming drug shipment. Then Oakland like you ordered," she said and sat on the edge of the bed. "That's how I knew you were planning on taking off, by the way. Why else would you let him handle everything?"

"Well, looks like you got your wish. I ain't going anywhere."

"Best decision ever." She grinned. "Wanna tell me what happened with that..." she swallowed whatever shit she was about to call

Cammie when my eyes flashed at her, "…that chick."

"No."

She sighed, still grinning, and got up. "Here's the thing about the Night Skulls. We don't hook up with outsiders. Normal people. That would never work. We gave up on *normal* so fucking long ago." She squeezed my shoulders. "I've seen that girl. She would've never fit in here anyway, baby. You gotta accept she was never yours."

Anger pulsed off me. Cammie was mine. I didn't give a shit what the whole world said. *Mine.* My fists clenched and unclenched during Mama's entire speech. When she finished, I shrugged her off me. "Gonna hit the shower."

"All right, sweetheart. I'm going." She kissed me on the cheek and left.

I pulled my T-shirt over my head and unbuckled my belt. As I unzipped my jeans, a knock on the door followed by Serena, one of Mama's favorite bitches, barging into my room, stopped me midway.

"What the fuck? I didn't tell you to come in," I yelled at the blonde.

Her crimson lips curved up, and her green eyes turned dark as they trailed down my naked abdomen along with the exposed rim of my boxers and then back to my chest.

"Need something?" I asked impatiently.

She sauntered toward me, her gaze dipping to my jeans. Then she ran her black-manicured fingers over my body. "I thought maybe *you* might be needing something."

I took her hands off me, my face contracting in disgust. "No thanks."

She thrust her perky tits up, and they threatened to bust out of her tiny, pink crop top. Then her hand finished unzipping my jeans and rested on my cock. "You sure about that?"

I smirked, my fingers tangling in her long hair. Her lips stretched from ear to ear, and her palm stroked me.

I leaned in, tightening my grip on her hair. She thought I was about to kiss her, but I reached her ear instead. "Tell Mama if she wanted to send a bitch to my room, she should've learned from Roar and sent a brunette. At least he knew what I preferred to fuck."

She moaned in pain. Panic flicked in her eyes when I met them. "Chill. I still haven't stooped that low to hit chicks." I let go of her hair. "Now take your ugly hand off my cock and get the fuck out."

"Yes, Dusty." Her heels clicked away quickly.

"Tell her what I said!"

"Yes, Dusty!" She ran faster and closed the door behind her.

A long, frustrated breath seeped out of my mouth. "Like she could get it up." Nobody knew or would believe that after Cammie, my cock got a one-track mind. A gorgeous brunette who could bring me to my knees and break me with both pain and pleasure.

No bitch was going to take her place.

CHAPTER 7

DUSTY

Aside from the regular business calls from suppliers, bars and other chapters, the rest of the weekend passed with the same shit. Party. Loads of booze, drugs and pussy. Sweetbutts, not just Mama's bitches, making passes at me—the newly-single president—aiming for higher privileges and status in the club. Mama trying to convince me Rosewood was where I belonged and Cammie could never be one of us.

I wanted to smash each and every face I saw in this place and then burn the whole thing to the ground.

To keep my angry episodes at bay, I spent a lot of time alone in the woods. I'd, compulsively, call Cammie without leaving a message. Then I'd drink and think about us. The good times and the bad ones. I'd never chased a girl before, never felt so…weak for a girl before, but Cameron Delaney wasn't any girl. She was the love of my life, the girl I wanted to spend my life with. A woman to die for.

Sometimes I wondered if our time together was limited from the start. Like no matter what I did, sooner or later she was going to leave. Like I was never going to be good enough, and she was better off without me.

Then I shook it off, knowing that was Mama's voice in my head. The effect of Rosewood on me. If those couple of days—staying here knowing I didn't have Cammie to go back to—made me realize anything, it was that I hated it here.

I was the one who could never fit here, Mama, not Cammie.

When I was forced by the Lanzas to take my position at the top of the Skulls, I always knew I'd find a way to leave one day. It was my time here that was limited, not my time with the one person that really made me feel like myself.

But all this time I wasn't worthy of her.

To get Cameron back, I had to prove myself to her, show her I wasn't full of shit when I said I'd change. I had to start over and build a new life on my own. It was the only way to redeem myself and regain her trust.

For that I would leave the Night Skulls once and for all and never look back. Show her I'd changed for good.

For myself.

For her.

For us.

I called Rush, determined to follow with my original plan, letting him subtly run things for a while to see if he was the right man for it before I went to Cosimo and made sure he understood I was leaving with no intention of running my own club or any club whatsoever. I'd called him that night I left Cammie and went to tell Rush about leaving and explained. He wasn't pleased, but he didn't object. He asked for a meet to sort things out.

I was ready to give him all the collateral he'd demand so I could go and be with Cammie. I had a feeling he wouldn't ask for a lot. Cosimo Lanza had been different since he married for love and his wife gave him a son. He'd understand, or I'd find a way, easy or hard, to make him understand.

Then I'd officially hand the whole business over to Rush. After all, he was the best candidate in the club for this position from the start. All brothers were on board when it came to VP.

He didn't answer, though. That was weird. Yes, he was busy following my orders. It didn't mean I wouldn't see or hear of him all weekend.

Something wasn't right.

CHAPTER 8

CAMERON

I summoned every ounce of courage left in me, backed up with Ashley's pep talk, and left the apartment to go to class.

The morning sun settled too bright on my puffy eyes as I put on my helmet, Hangovers and mornings didn't get along. Crying all night didn't help either.

Ash put on the extra helmet while I jammed dark shades on my face and straddled the bike. I could only wear one glove today. The glove on the right hand didn't fit after last night's little accident. The handlebar didn't feel rough on the gauze anyway.

Taking a deep breath, I tried to stop the racing thoughts in my mind, and most importantly, not to think about Dusty. But with riding the bike he gave me—riding or seeing any bike for that matter—it was impossible.

My best friend held on to my shoulders, and as if she felt my tension, she said, "Don't think too much. Just drive."

I nodded, filling my lungs with air, and started the ignition. The fresh air and the rush helped calm me a little. We reached campus on time, and I parked the Harley at its regular spot. Without taking off my shades, I walked with Ash to class, grateful she wasn't embarrassed to be associated with me.

I shoved my hands in the pockets of my jeans, my eyes darting around, bracing for the worst, but to my surprise, we reached our building in peace. Apart from the few eye daggers that fell on us as we climbed the stairs, nothing happened.

"See? Not as bad as you thought," Ash said.

"Yeah. Don't know what I expected. Guess I have an inflated ego or something to think people would be occupied by what happened on my account."

She laughed and pushed the class door open. A small smile tugged at my lips, but as the buzz inside the classroom faded when we entered, so did my smile.

I walked quickly to an empty row in the back, Ash on my tail. The few eyes daggers earlier were nothing compared to the ones everybody was giving me here. And that wasn't even a class I shared with Samuel.

Humming whispers and swears flew around. "The fuck? How can she still be here? They should expel her."

"They almost killed the guy."

"She's got a lot of nerve showing up here."

Ash and I took our seats. I did my best to ignore the continuous word slashes.

A girl in the row in front of me looked at my injured hand over her shoulder and then back to her friend. "Did that jerk hit her too? Or was she beating that poor guy with him?"

"Ignore them," Ash said, patting my thigh.

Was what had happened not hideous enough? They were spreading more terrible rumors? I chewed on my lips, angry, nervous…guilty.

Professor Lahey entered. Finally. His presence paused the gossip but not the pointed looks or the hate notes. Yes. Pieces of paper kept flying to my bench as if we were in high school or something. Against my better judgment, I opened one of them.

Go back to your gang, bitch.

My cheeks burned as I exhaled a troubled breath. I reached for another note.

Lucky I never asked you out, or I'd be dead by now. You're too ugly anyway. I didn't need to read the rest of the god-awful things my classmates thought of me.

Ash pushed them all out of my way with her arm like trash. "Don't read that. I'll throw them all away," she whispered.

I shook my head, my chest heaving with anger. "Don't you dare."

Perhaps I got involved with the wrong guy, and a not-so-innocent man had to suffer because of it. That didn't give anyone the right to bully me. Even if I felt as guilty as Dusty for Samuel's beating, I wouldn't tolerate that kind of treatment.

As soon as the class was dismissed, I shoved all the notes in my pocket and barged outside, heading for the Dean's office.

Ashley ran after me. "Cameron, wait. I'm coming with you."

"No. Go to your class. I'll deal with this on my own."

"C'mon. Don't be like this. I'm—"

"Go to class!" My fists balled, and I immediately regretted my behavior. I paused and held her shoulders. "I'm sorry. I didn't mean to yell at you like this."

"No worries, babe. You're angry. I get it. I'd be angry, too. We're good."

"Thank you."

"No need to escalate things, though. These assholes will find something else to keep their knuckleheads busy soon. All this will fade with time. But if you make a big deal out of it, you might get burned for something you didn't even do."

"Maybe. But I refuse to spend the next few months in this shit. I must do something or I'll wind up—"

"Delaney!" A male voice shouted behind me, interrupting me. My head whipped toward it, and I saw it was one of my classmates. "It's your bike," he continued. "They're trashing it."

"Son of a…" I ran off to the parking lot, but by the time I arrived, whoever vandalized my bike was gone.

My hands clasped behind the back of my head as I stared at the damage, panting. The bike was covered with trash and spit. Drops of yellow liquid trickled from the seat on the ground. I couldn't tell if it was soda or piss.

And the words 'gangster whore' were sprayed along the side in red paint.

I wanted to cry. I wanted to scream.

To destroy.

"What the fuck?" Ash exclaimed.

Rage thundered inside me, pounding my head. "Still think I should just stand by and let it fade with time?"

CHAPTER 9

CAMERON

The Dean's words echoed in my ears as I stampeded out of his office.

We understand your frustration, and we can assure you we'll investigate the matter thoroughly, Miss Delaney. However, without enough witnesses, there's so much we can do. If you prefer to get the police involved for better results, we'd be happy to assist you further.

The police? The ones who set the murderer of my sister free on the same day he was arrested? Or the ones who protected the business of gangs like The Night Skulls for their benefit?

Even if the police could bring me justice this time, the Dean was saying it as a threat not as a viable option to consider. As if he was saying Samuel didn't press charges, and I'd better do the same.

What had I expected anyway? I was so stupid to think for a second he would behave differently. On days like these, it seemed that Dusty's logic was the only kind that made sense.

I left school on foot, still figuring out what to do about the bike. Wandering outside the gates, I found a Harley by the curb, a man with a gray beard on top of it, the patch on the back of his cut unmistakable.

The Night Fucking Skulls.

He got off his bike when he saw me, and I got a closer look at him. Big, tattooed and familiar. The helmet and sunglasses hid most of his face, but I recognized him.

Rush, Dusty's VP.

I strode over to him. "What's wrong? Is Dusty all right?"

He crossed his arms over his chest, the flexing muscles making him look even bigger, and leaned his back on the bike. "He's fine."

"Then what are you doing here?" I studied his face suspiciously. His tone, despite being calm and nonchalant, triggered an invisible alarm in me. "Are you following me?"

"Only following orders. He sent me here to keep an eye on you."

"Well, tell him I'm fine. I don't need a bodyguard. As you can see I'm capable of staying in one piece on my own."

His head lowered, and I assumed he was looking at my hand. "What happened here?"

"Nothing serious."

He grunted. "And where's your ride?"

I groped for a palpable lie. If I told him the truth, he'd tell Dusty. This time, Dusty would kill somebody for real. "Didn't feel like riding today."

"I see." He straightened up and gestured for me to get on his bike. "How about I give you a ride home?"

That was an intriguing offer since I didn't have one anymore. I took a couple of steps forward, but that invisible alarm in me blew in my head. For some reason, I thought about Annie and how she had been abducted.

On a bike just like this one. By a Night Skull like the one standing before me. His former president to be exact. This situation was completely different, but somehow it felt the same.

I stepped back. "I'll pass."

"C'mon, Dusty is gonna kill me if he knows I let you go alone like that."

"He knows I can take care of myself. Thanks for offering anyway." I wheeled away as fast as I could.

CHAPTER 10

DUSTY

Mama,

I wish I could stay here and be the leader of the family you love so much. Sorry to disappoint you, but I've made up my mind. I'm going to SLO to be with Cammie. I love her. She's the only person that's keeping me sane in this mess.

Don't worry. Even though my time here is done, my successor, whoever he'll be, is going to protect you as if I was here and never left.

I love you, Mama. I'll always make sure you're safe.

Wish me luck.

Dusty

I folded the note and put it on the nightstand next to my bed. My already-packed backpack flung on my shoulder. Helmet under my arm. Weapons, boots and cut on. Money in wallet. I was good to go.

After my meet with Cosimo last night, there was nothing that held me back anymore. As long as I didn't start any clubs of my own or got in the way of business, Cosimo had no problem with my not being Prez anymore. It helped that his wife and Cammie used to be friends. He also said he knew what it meant to change for the woman you loved, to be ready to give up everything for her.

I reached Cal Poly around four p.m., hoping I'd catch my Cammie as she left campus. She was still not answering her phone.

Impatience beat me after a few minutes of waiting, so I decided to call Ashley. Maybe I'd have better luck there.

"Hello?" she answered.

"Hey, Ash. It's me…Dusty." I wet my lips. "Uh…how you doing?"

A sigh. "What do you want?"

"Ouch. Does that mean you hate me, too?"

"What do you want, Dusty?"

"Well…is Cammie with you? I tried to call her so many times, but she never picks up."

"That's because she gave me her phone, precisely so she won't do that."

I nodded, blowing a breath out in frustration. "I get it. Fuck. Um…is she with you now by any chance?"

"No. She took off early. I'm still at school."

I ran a thumb over my eyebrow, shaking my head. "Okay. Can I see you for a second? I'm right outside, by the way."

"Dusty, I don't know."

"Please, Ash."

A long pause.

"C'mon. You're my last hope. Please."

Another sigh. "Fine. I'll be out in a minute."

Yes! "Thank you."

I took off my helmet and rested against the bike until she came out. A scowl on her little face. Her arms stiff. Her eyes wary.

"Shit. I was hoping when you see me, you'll forgive me and like me again." I plastered my best crooked smile on my lips.

She shrugged. "You've been a dick. Your charms don't work when you've been a dick."

"True. And I understand if you don't wanna be seen with me, especially here. Do you wanna go somewhere?"

"No. Just say what you're here for. You gotta know I'm not gonna be your messenger, though. I'm on Cam's side on this, and I'll protect my girl even from you."

"Fair enough." I put my hands together in a plea. "Can you please tell me if she's gonna be home tonight?"

"Where else would she be? Today was the first day she left the apartment after that stupid Valentine's and look what happened to…" She chopped off her words.

My body jerked upright away from the bike, the beast inside me clawing up. "What happened to her?"

"Oh fuck."

"What happened?" I snarled. "Is she fucking all right?"

"Yeah, yeah. It's just…" She filled me in on the notes and the bike. My fists and teeth clenched, and my blood simmered by the second as I listened.

She stared at me with a warning in her eyes. "You're gonna do something stupid again, aren't you?"

My demons played with my head. Yes, I wanted to hurt every bastard who thought they could mess with my ol'lady. But I knew if I did that again, Cameron would hate me forever. I was trying to win her back not lose her.

"Fuck!" Taking a deep breath, I tried to let go of my anger and pride for a minute. "No." I shook my head, convincing myself before her. "Not this time."

"Good."

"All right. I'll take care of the bike. If it's finished by tonight, I'll swing by and bring it to your place." If I fixed things instead of destroying them, maybe Cammie would see that I was changing and give me a chance. "Could you do me this one favor and tell her I've moved to SLO?"

She cocked a brow at me. "Did ya?"

"Yes, and I'm not going anywhere."

"But you're still wearing your cut and patch."

"There are some rules to lose those. I can't just take them off and say bye-bye. There will be Church and a vote, and then an unceremonious slicing of my colors off my cut, usually followed by spit, curses and death threats."

"That doesn't sound pleasant." She bit her lip on a smile.

"It's the worst, but enough about the club." I pleaded with my eyes. "Will you tell her? Pretty please."

Her smile turned into a grin. "I can do that...or, maybe, I can go out for drinks around nine-ish and stupidly forget to lock the door so *someone* even stupider can show up and tell her himself?"

I'd crush her in a bear hug if Cammie didn't get jealous of even those innocent hugs. I chuckled. "Much *stupider*, yes."

"Um-hum."

"Thank you so much, Ash. You're a really good friend."

"And you're trouble." She spun and started back to campus. "Huge, hot, fucking gorgeous trouble."

"I heard that."

She flipped me off. "Don't blow it."

CHAPTER 11

CAMERON

"Can I come with?" I asked Ash when she told me she was going out tonight.

"Uh...really?"

I shrugged. "Probably not a good idea, but I don't want to be alone. Today has been more than stressful. I don't want to spend the rest of it brooding or overthinking."

Her lashes fluttered. "Yeah...sure."

Why was she nervous all of a sudden? She'd been badgering me about going out, and now that I said yes, she didn't want me to go? Maybe after the vandalism she was scared or didn't want whoever she was going out with to see me with her. Or see me at all. Who would blame her? I was a walking hazard now.

"You know what? I changed my mind." I spun toward my room. "I feel really tired. I shouldn't be drinking anyway."

"Cameron, don't get mad at me. I have a feeling you'll be happier here tonight."

What did that even mean? I glanced at her over my shoulder, noticing the wiggly dance she did when she was excited and the smile she was trying to conceal.

"What are you hiding from me, Ash?"

She did an invisible zip over her mouth. "Sorry. You'll know in a few minutes." She sprinted to the door but then twisted back. "What do you mean you shouldn't drink?"

My breath accelerated in my chest. I opened my mouth, but the words refused to come out. I pressed my lips shut and shrugged, tears pricking my eyes.

She gaped at me endlessly, and then she slapped a hand over her mouth. "Oh my God, oh my God, oh my GOD!"

"I was too distraught after the breakup I forgot to take the pill. I don't know for sure, though. For now, I'm just late," I mumbled.

"Just late?! The fuck? Do you want me to bring you a test?"

"I…I…uh…I don't think I'm ready to know yet."

"Why the fuck not? Cam, this is big. Knowing early is better if, you know, you decide not to keep it."

My arms circled around my abdomen protectively as my brows hooked. A tightness in my heart labored my breath.

"You want to keep it, don't you?"

"Would it be so bad if I did?"

A tender smile stretched her lips before she ran toward me and gave me a hug. "No, babe. It's not so bad. It's not bad at all."

"Dusty is a dangerous man. An outlaw. I don't want his life for our baby…but I won't be able to do this without him."

"Just ask yourself one question. If you're pregnant, will that make you happy?"

I nodded through the tears. "But I feel so guilty about it."

"Don't be. You're allowed to be happy about having a baby even when the father is questionable, and infuriatingly sexy. Fuck, who wouldn't want to have that fire, assholish sex god's baby? I'd kill for his genes alone. Fuck me, I'd ride his huge, badass pierced dick until I die not just until he puts a baby in my belly."

I held her tight, laughing and crying at the same time. "I don't know what I'd do without you, Ash."

"You'll do just fine." She pecked my cheek and drew back. "You really need that test, though. I wanna know if I'm gonna be an auntie. But don't do it now. Save it till the end of the night."

"What? Why?"

"Trust me. I have a feeling tonight is gonna turn into a much better night than you think, and if you save that test till the end, it's gonna be epic." She did her excited dance as she bolted to the door.

I stood there for a few seconds. What the hell just happened? *What are you up to, you crazy little thing?* I laughed under my breath and sat on the couch, something lumpy under my butt. I grabbed it and saw it was Ashley's purse. She forgot it while she literally ran to God-knew where.

She probably forgot to lock the door, too. I didn't hear the keys, which were most likely in her purse.

I rose to my feet and ambled to check. Before my hand reached the knob, the door banged my forehead violently, knocking me down on the floor.

"What the fuck?" I gasped. As I looked up, a huge man in a black ski mask towered over me.

His gloved hands grabbed me from my shirt and lifted me in the air. My eyes bulged in panic, my mind racing blank. I was too confused and stunned to understand what the hell was going on.

He pinned me to the wall with one hand around my neck and kicked the door shut. Then he slapped me.

Each blow from the back of his hand whipped my head so fast my vision was compromised. But the pain and the taste of blood in my mouth snapped me out of shock.

I began to register little pieces of information about the assailant. He was covered in black leather and denim from head to toe. His eyes were the only things I could see. Green. Oddly familiar.

"Dusty?" I choked.

His hand clenched into a punching fist. A hazy glimpse of a skull tattoo appeared on the little area on his wrist that was exposed. It was different from the one Dusty had, but it was definitely Night Skull ink.

My jaws clicked at the first punch. It banged right through my head like a dinner gong. One more of these, and I'd pass out. Time to do something. Anything.

My limbs moved all at once, flailing in the air, hitting whatever part of him they reached. It distracted him for a second that his grip around my neck loosened, allowing me more air, and I gathered all my strength to shoot my knee up, swift and hard.

He grunted as I made contact with his balls, and I fell off his grasp. "Bitch!"

That voice. That grunt. I knew it.

Oh my God. That was Rush.

I crawled away from him as fast as I could, my mind too clouded to figure out why Dusty's VP came here to beat me up. Didn't Dusty send him for my protection?

It doesn't matter now! Adrenaline and self-preservation screamed at me. I clutched at the doorknob with both hands, lifting myself up to escape. Trying to overpower a man like Rush in a fight was an act of madness.

His heavy hands fell on my shoulders and yanked me across the room. My back crushed against the cold surface of the coffee table. The sharp edges poked me before I heard the glass shatter and stab me like a million pins at once.

I screamed. Then I did it again much louder, crying for help, realizing it was an option I was too shocked to utilize from the start.

"Shut the fuck up." He swooped down on me. More blows rained on my face. My eyes swelled, almost closing. Then he got something out of his pocket and shoved it in my mouth. "You're making this way too hard than it should be."

The rubber taste and the stretch of my jaws and cheeks as he tied something behind my head confirmed that was a ball gag in my mouth. My screams came out muffled as I pounded his chest with my fists, my knee aiming for another shot at his nuts.

He tried to pin me down as he straddled my hips, but I swiftly pushed myself backwards and put all my force to roll over on my stomach. I wanted to get up and make a run for the door, but his fingers tangled in my hair, pulling it hard.

"Where the fuck you think you're going?" he growled, his grip tight in my hair, shaking my whole body with his yanks. "You're mine now, bitch."

What? His? What the fuck was going on?

"Sorry. I don't mean to interrupt anything." Ashley's voice streamed from outside, and then her feet blurred on the threshold. "I forgot my…b…ag."

No. No. NO. NO! My heart thrashed, and Rush swore.

She froze, staring vacantly at Rush. "You're not Dusty."

"Ashley, run! RUN!" I cried out at the top of my lungs so she could understand me.

Her eyes flashed at me for a split-second before she darted away.

"Shit. This's gonna get very messy now." He dragged me while he went after her. His free hand reached in the back of his jeans and got out a gun. Then he stretched his arm toward running Ashley.

"No! Leave her alone, you son of a bitch!" I elbowed him in the stomach, and dragged myself up to my feet. Then I kicked him in the shin and stomped on his foot.

It didn't stop or even shake him.

Ashley couldn't make it to the end of the hallway before the muffled gunshot pelted my ear and the bullet landed in her head.

CHAPTER 12

CAMERON

I lost my sister all over again. That was how I felt as Ashley's hair swam in crimson blood.

Rush dragged me around and scooped Ash's body off the floor as if she weighed nothing. Her blood left a trail back to the apartment.

He dropped her inside without a care in the world and shut the door. "Someone is gonna call the cops now. Gotta get this done fast." He dropped me so roughly I thought my nose broke when it hit the ground.

I was already in too much pain to feel any new strikes. Numb from the inside out. My mind played tricks on me that I thought I was in one of my nightmares, and it would be over as soon as I woke up.

But it was real. Ashley's death was real.

Rush, tearing my pants from behind now, was real.

"I'd knock you out, but I need you broken over this." He flipped me over, and I heard the jingling of a belt buckle. My eyes were too swollen to see it for sure.

He ripped off my panties. "For the record, I wasn't planning on killing anyone tonight. If you'd come with me after school like I told you, she would've still been alive."

My gut feeling was right to walk away from him when he offered me a ride. He was planning to kidnap me all along. I wished I hadn't listened and let him kidnap me. At least, Ashley would have still been alive. And now this...

My eyes twitched and throbbed as I felt his weight on top of me and his hand around my throat. As he was about to mount me.

Two choices flashed in my head.

One: drift in the darkness threatening to swallow me and let him do what he came here to do.

Two: do everything in my power to stop the son of a bitch. No matter what.

Something flared in me, a strength I didn't know I still had left or the colossal hate I had for the Night fucking Skulls. All I knew was that if I was going down, letting those fuckers win again wasn't an option. The second choice seemed so much more appealing.

I crashed my forehead against his chest as hard as I could. Once. Twice. Three times. He backed off a little, struggling to breathe. Then my knee shot up, hitting his hanging nuts with a crack.

"Not again, you bitch!" He plopped on his back with a loud thud, cupping his crotch, growling.

I jumped to my feet. Well, I tried. His hand reached for my ankle, bringing me back down. I kicked, freeing myself but stumbling into the couch. I crept away from him on the cold floor, glass splinters spearing me, going inside of me, my hands desperate for anything I could use as a weapon.

"Damn, you're feisty." The glass clinked under his weight as he went after me from behind. "No wonder he fell hard for you. I like feisty brunettes, too."

In a swift move, my shirt, the last piece of clothing covering me, tore with a loud ripping sound under his hands. He held my wrists and pressed them to the floor as he flipped me on my back. "Like father like son."

"What?" I gasped through the gag.

"You haven't figured it out yet? Dusty was never Roar's. He's always been mine."

Nauseated and shocked, I strained my eyes to stare at his. They looked exactly like Dusty's I'd mistaken Rush for him earlier. Except they were menacing and brutal and cold, and now they were filled with predatory rage and lust.

The sick revelation dawned on me sending a stronger wave of nausea down my core. A man raping his kid's girlfriend was a new level of sick shit only the Night Skulls were capable of hitting.

"Not that I want you for myself, but I have to do this." He placed my wrists on top of each other above my head and held them with one grip, the other securing his gun behind him and then lowering his jeans. "I know your type. You can't be with him after I have my way with you, and he wouldn't touch you again knowing he couldn't protect you." He pulled out his penis. "Nothing personal. It's the only way you'd leave him the fuck alone so he remains President."

What the fuck? That was all they cared about? Killing Ashley, raping me, breaking and fucking their own president's life just to protect their business? I squirmed, lying beneath him, hope slipping out of me. "He'll kill you."

"What? Kill me like he killed Roar for you? Is that what you said?" He chuckled. The fucking bastard chuckled. "He can't. There's a lot you don't know, but I'll tell you this. He won't make the same mistake twice. I made sure of it."

What the fuck did that mean? My mind raced to find an answer but then stopped to a halt when the horrors of the time I'd spent in Rosewood while Roar tried to rape me assaulted me as hard as Rush was doing to me now. The tip of his penis penetrated me, and I was so tense I couldn't even piss myself to stop him. I spat, aiming for his face, forgetting I was gagged, and drool streamed down my chin instead of his face. He watched me, his eyes oozing with evil joy.

Choice one seemed appropriate now. I'd fought and fought but was overpowered by the Night Skulls. I lost. In fact, I'd lost the battle against them from the day they took Annie. Everything I did was for nothing. I lost my sister and my family. I lost Dusty. I lost Ashley. I was about to lose my life too. I closed the little crack of my eyes that was still open and surrendered to the blackness about to engulf me.

The world stopped for a moment. No noises. No pain.

Stillness.

Surrender.

Peace.

Then, right before the last shred of resistance left my body, Annie's image flashed in the back of my head.

Then Roar's.

Ashley's bloody corpse.

Rush's face.

I screamed against the gag from the bottom of my heart, all the pain and the loss and rage flooding to the surface all at once. My eyes strained to look at that monster in reality. His evil laughter echoed, but then his voice morphed into a more pleasant one. Dusty's.

"Get the fuck off her!" I heard him say. Then a click. A gun click. "Now!"

Suddenly, the weight pressing over me vanished. My eyes barely opened at my command, and Dusty was standing at the door, over Ashley's body.

Rush mumbled something to Dusty, but I couldn't hear it. One voice boomed inside me. Took over me in a way that made it impossible to hear anything else.

Some fuckers deserve to die. It's a necessity.

As if it had a mind of its own, my hand grabbed Rush's gun from the back of his jeans. The son of a bitch's head jerked toward me, and I aimed with whatever vision I had left.

"Cammie, no!" Dusty shouted.

I pulled the trigger. As many times as I could.

CHAPTER 13

DUSTY

My head rested on my palm while I sat in an armchair next to my bed, my gaze trailing back and forth between Cammie's bruised, closed eyelids, her swollen lips and her chest.

Waiting.

She'd passed out after she fired that gun and hadn't opened her eyes since. Owl, our Doc brother and my best friend, said she'd been in coma since the attack. It'd been two days since I moved her to Rosewood. Even if she was going to hate me for it when she woke up, it was the safest place to be at the moment.

I rubbed my tired eyes, my body begging me to go to sleep. But I couldn't. Even when I lay next to her, forcing myself to rest, I was haunted by what happened to her.

Because of me.

It was the middle of the night. The partying had cooled down since I'd returned. What happened to Rush—what Rush had done— left us all in a…pensive mode.

How could he do that to my woman when he'd known I was his son all this time? How did he think there would be no retaliation when he was one of the very few that knew I shot Roar for the very same thing he was doing to Cammie?

Stillness fell over the room, nothing but her breath dancing with mine and the beeping machine as I watched her, recalling, regretting, grieving. I still had no idea how I was going to tell her about…

My heart squeezed as I remembered the conversation I had with Owl.

"Why isn't she waking up?" I'd asked.

"I don't know. I cleaned all her wounds. Made sure there were no glass shards anywhere in her body. There was no internal bleeding, thank fuck. All her vitals are good. Apart from the broken nose, the contusions and the battering, she's physically stable, but she's been seriously traumatized. Everybody reacts differently to trauma."

"What's that mean? Is she ever going to wake up?"

"Most likely, yes. We just don't know when."

"What's with all that blood down there? I stopped Rush before he raped her. That can't be from the glass splinters, right?"

"No. There wasn't much inside to begin with, and I took them all out. All her inner wounds are superficial."

"Then what the fuck was that?"

"I'm sorry, Dusty. She was..."

"Was what?"

"I'm afraid she was pregnant. The trauma has induced a miscarriage."

My tears betrayed me now as they did when he'd told me the first time. If it was that hard on me, how would it be on her?

A faint knock on the door snapped me out of my thoughts. I wiped my face quickly. "Come in."

"Hey, Prez." Owl entered. "Just going to check on her real quick."

I was so grateful for Owl. Not only for taking care of Cammie and bringing every medical equipment she needed here instead of having to take her to a fucking hospital, but also because he helped me charter a plane real fast, which took us back to Rosewood after the attack in no time.

That old man used to be a good ER doctor at County and only rode for fun. If he hadn't been so fixed on painkillers, he would've done way better outside. But everybody was fixed on something, and he loved drugs and Harleys.

As far as I knew, after he finished his miles, earned his patch and went by Owl as his road name a couple of months ago, I'd never seen him happier.

"Is she getting any better?" I asked as he moved his flashlight pen thing over her eyes.

"The swelling is better. All these bruises will be gone in a week or so. The scars on her back will be nastier than the old ones, though." He stood to replace the bag on her IV.

The old ones were caused by Roar. The new ones by Rush. My precious fathers.

Mama had told me the truth when we got back. That cunt had been more devastated about Rush's death than what he'd done to my girl. And when I told her I'd lost my unborn baby because of him, I didn't see empathy or sadness in her eyes. I saw panic. Real fear.

That got me suspicious she was behind this shit all along. When she took off that very same hour, I knew for sure.

She couldn't run away forever. I would find her. I would make her pay.

She did everything in her power to make me President. I would show her what the Nigh Skull's President did to back-stabbing cunts like her.

As soon as Cammie woke up.

If she ever did.

CHAPTER 14

DUSTY

Blood splattered on my jeans and boots as I slammed my fist into the side of Pat's head. The sniveling junkie piled into a heap on the cement floor of the Boiler—the Night Skulls' torture room. Each chapter had one of those, even in Europe.

He climbed to his knees. "Please, Prez. I swear I don't know where she is." His shaking hands laced together like he was praying. Prayer couldn't help him now.

With an unforgiving backhand, I laid him flat. "You were the only fucker Beth was spotted with before she disappeared. You know where she's hiding, and you're going to tell me all about it."

Surrounded by cigarette butts, empty beer cans, and dead cockroaches such as himself if he didn't come clean in the next minute, Pat lay, unmoving in the dark. They always thought if they could fake unconsciousness, the beating would stop.

They were wrong.

I glanced to my side at Big Gun, my Enforcer. He stood a foot taller than I was, his huge arms crossed over his chest, his bald head sweating under the one lit lamp hanging from the ceiling in this old utility room. Then I nodded at the tool bench across from me.

Big Gun scanned the instruments scattered atop it and picked up pliers with dried blood covering them. "Pulling some teeth will get him talking."

The whimpering puddle got to his feet before Big Gun even stepped to pull him up. "No, no! Fuck this shit. I'm your man, Prez. I'd never—"

My fist connected with his jaws, sending a tooth flying out already. His head cracked to the side, and he groaned, spitting out blood.

I grabbed his neck and pressed him to the wall, and then punched him in the stomach.

His knees gave, and he drooled blood on the floor. "Take over, Big Gun," I ordered.

The fucking junkie trembled as my Enforcer approached with the pliers. Pat's swollen eyes widened when Big Gun yanked the pliers open and shoved them in the fucker's mouth. Pat mumbled his protest, choking. Then he said something in panic. A name.

On my silent order, Big Gun removed the tool from the guy's mouth. "Speak, bitch."

"Wrench," Pat spat, his rancid breath mixed with the scent of blood filling my nostrils. "Mama needed help to go to Wrench."

I cocked a brow. Wrench was the VP of the Detroit chapter and Roar's best friend. When *she* killed Roar, Wrench was the first to launch a crusade down here, demanding the cunt was killed. It took a massive gun deal delivered to him to shut him up.

"You're lying." I nodded at Big Gun again.

The sharp edge of the pliers hit Pat's teeth. He jerked his head and shook it fast, bloody spit spraying right and left. "No, no, I swear. I arranged for the ride myself."

"You helped her out of the state?" I snarled.

He stilled as he suddenly realized what he'd said. "It's not what you think, Prez! I swear I didn't know you had beef with her then."

I stared into his glazed, half-open eyes, making sure he understood I wasn't fucking around.

"That's all I know. I'd never lie to you, Prez," he stammered. Then he started crying.

Fine. He wasn't lying. He was just a stupid fuck who believed that snake bitch. A junkie who would do anything for blow.

He fell to my boots, begging for mercy. I kicked him off me and started for the back door. "Church in five. And tell one of the prospects to grab a mop and clean up here," I told Big Gun.

"No, no, no!" Pat screamed and whimpered like a little bitch. "I'm sorry. Please—"

Bang!

I didn't have to look back to know that his blood and brain matter flew over and splattered on the floor.

CHAPTER 15

DUSTY

I took the back exit and headed straight to the clubhouse. If I set foot inside the house, I wouldn't be able to stop myself from checking on Cammie, and that would take hours. If it were for me, I'd stay with her all day and all night until she woke up.

But I was doing all this for her. I had to find the cunt that set my VP, my real father, to rape my ol'lady and drive her away from me. The bitch behind the murder of my unborn child.

For the fire blazing inside me, consuming what was left of my heart and soul, to die, for

Cammie to be safe and for us to live in peace as my ol'lady always wanted, Beth had to die.

I wouldn't rest until I sent her to the hell she belonged to.

I stepped into the clubhouse, weed and cigarette smoke greeting me, music cranked up at its loudest. A few men were over at the pool table, laughing, holding their beers. A blonde lay on her back on the table, topless, spread eagle, an eight ball over her belly button, and one of the guys was aiming to shoot it with his stick. Except the stick was his cock and the hole was her mouth.

A bunch of brothers were hanging with their whores at the bar. In the middle of the clubhouse, prospects along with Owl—no longer just Doc now but our newly-appointed Treasurer after Beth ran off—sank in the leather couches, watching a couple of club skanks stripping and pole dancing.

The world might turn upside down, but the party never stopped in Rosewood. Well, it slowed down for a couple of days after what Rush and Beth had done, but that was all the Night Skulls could handle.

"Church, now," I yelled over the music and headed up the stairs. Owl followed, and Skid, the Road Captain, emerged from the bar. By the time I reached the top of the stairs, Big

Gun was entering the clubhouse and telling a prospect to clean up the mess in the Boiler.

I unlocked Church and took my seat at the head of the table. Owl and Skid took their places as well. Then Big Gun closed the door and sat next to me.

"The number of people allowed to this table keeps shrinking," I said. Despite everything, not having Rush and Mam—Beth—here was hard to get used to.

Owl scratched his grey beard. "You really need to appoint a new VP, Prez. Now."

"I'm being betrayed right and left. You really think this is the time to get someone new here? No. Besides, we have a more pressing matter to deal with." My stare shifted around the three men. "As you all now, Beth was spotted with that fucking junkie at the Little Wicked, our own titty bar, right after she took off. According to him she was trying to reach Wrench."

"The fucking shit she was." Skid rested his elbows on the table, the skulls on his biceps bulging, his long, ginger hair covering half of his face. "Mama might be a lot of things, but she ain't stupid. The piece of shit was lying."

"Beth," I corrected. "That bitch lost her name the second she set a hit on my ol'lady."

He nodded. "Sure, Prez."

Sliding in my seat, I rested my head back and sighed. "He wasn't lying. But you're right, she ain't stupid. She knew I'd get to that fucker, and he'd tell me what she wanted me to know. A decoy so I'd be sidetracked while she found her way out."

"You think she'll hide at another chapter or she'll leave the country?" Owl asked.

"She hasn't left the country yet, that I know. Airports are a no go unless she wants the pigs after her, and I set men on the lookout on every border," Big Gun said. The man didn't speak much, but when he did, he knew his shit.

I rubbed my exhausted eyes and shifted my body upwards. "The only lead we have now is that ride. Gotta find out where she was actually dropped off and where she headed after."

Skid slammed his hands together in a loud clap. "Let's hit the road."

"Go with him, Big. Won't hurt to send some prospects to sniff around Detroit, too."

"Done." Big Gun left his seat, and Skid followed. The two men, almost the same height, blocked the light as they stood. Except for the patches and the hair, as they walked to the door with their full sleeves and cuts, they looked like twins.

I hit the gavel announcing the end of Church. "And brothers…"

They both turned to me.

"I need her alive when you find her."

"Sure thing, Prez," Skid said while Big Gun nodded.

Taking a deep breath, imagining the horrors I'd do to that bitch when they brought her to me, I wiped my face with my hands as they closed the door behind them.

"You seriously need a rest." Owl fished a joint out of his pocket and handed it to me. "You haven't slept in three days."

I lit the joint and rose to my feet. "I'll rest when I'm dead."

He made a sound in the back of his throat that was supposed to be a laugh. "There's no rest for us then, son."

He had a point.

Still, I couldn't rest even if I wanted to. Not with Cammie like this. I drew a long breath of weed smoke and handed the joint back to him. "I'll go check on my ol'lady."

A smile showed the two wrinkles around the corners of his mouth. "Keep it. I'll light my own." His hand went through his pocket again as he stood. "Holler if you need anything."

CHAPTER 16

DUSTY

Metal music loud enough to wake the dead
but not my Cammie poured from two large
speakers in the front yard. Watching the men
climb onto their bikes and roar off in single
file, I sat on the porch to finish the joint
before I went to my room. I couldn't risk this
shit reaching Cammie's brain in that state.

Eight prospects and three Rottweilers
guarded the gates as they closed. A few
brothers sat around the fire with beers and
whiskey by the dry pool. They were helping
themselves to a couple of Beth's bitches,
Serena and Candy, and a young hangaround.

One of the brothers, Chain, nearly tripped over his feet as he signaled for me to join them.

I shook my head and dragged another breath from the joint.

"Why the fuck not? You've been dry for weeks." He laughed.

Since Halloween to be exact. But the only lips and pussy I was desperate to have around my cock had been bruised and aching, and their owner, *my* owner, was in a coma in my bed, not knowing I was even there.

The hangaround, couldn't be over seventeen, jumped to her feet and strutted my way, her big tits—too big for her age to be real—bouncing in her tank top. Her shorts were too short and so tight I could see the outline of her pussy from here.

"No, Zoey. Prez is off-limits!" someone yelled.

She ignored them, and with a grin, she tried to settle into my lap.

I pushed her aside. "You should've listened. There's plenty of dick around to give you what you came here for."

A scowl replaced her grin. Her brown hair brushed my arms as she eased down on the porch next to me. "Why so pissed?"

My two fathers tried to rape and kill the love of my life and died in the process. My unborn child was dead because of my pathetic excuse of a mother. She is now on the run and I have to hunt her down to off her. And my ol'lady, the only good person in my life that hasn't been tainted by blood, has turned killer overnight and has been in a fucking coma since.

"Go back to your friends."

"I have something better in mind." She got on her knees.

When her hands touched my thighs, I slapped off her wrists. "What the fuck? Just go."

"What?" She looked like she was about to cry.

"You heard me, bitch. The next time I slap you it will be on your fucking cunt face. Go!"

Tears pricked her brown eyes as she collected herself up and ran back to the bonfire. I hated it when I had to pull something like this, but sometimes it was the only way to keep them the fuck off.

"Don't blubber, darling. Dusty only has cock for Sleeping Beauty," Serena said, Chain motorboating her.

Sucking in the last breath of this joint, I gestured for her to come here with my index finger. She stood so fast Chain fell to his side.

Unbothered to cover her tits, she hurried to me. "You need anything, Dusty?" she asked seductively, her pink nipples as hard as pebbles. She thrust her chest up for a better view, her flesh red. Her shoulders and jaws were tense, though, and I could easily hear the fear in her voice. She must have been recalling our last encounter when Beth had sent her to my room to make me forget all about Cammie.

"Get on your knees," I ordered, throwing away the joint butt.

A sparkle hit her green eyes. Her bright red lips stretched from ear to ear as her knees rested between my feet.

"Way to go, Serena. Service Prez good. Get him the fuck out of the monastery," someone yelled, and laughter flew in the air.

She reached for my belt, her dirty blonde hair touching my jeans. "My pleasure."

I smirked at her. "Where's Beth, Serena?"

Her hands stopped midway. "What?"

"I get she was in a hurry running for her life to take her bitches with her. But you're her favorite." I leaned forward, holding her gaze so she knew I wasn't fucking around. "She must have told you something, gave you a name or a number to call in case you needed her."

Blood slid from her face, leaving her as white as the dead. "She left without a word or a warning. We woke up and found her gone just like you."

I yanked hard at her hair, straining her neck backwards. She gasped and moaned in pain. "Dusty, I work for the Night Skulls, not for Mama. I'm your girl. I already told you I don't know shit. I'd never lie to you."

"You lie for a living, you whore." I pulled her hair so hard I felt some of it come off in my grip. Then I got my knife out and ran its flat side on her cheek. "Maybe a nice scar on this pretty face will get you speaking."

"I'm your best working girl here, Prez. A scar would put me out of business. *Your* business," she whimpered.

"And I'd do it with a huge fucking smile. Start singing, bitch."

"You know better than anyone Mama never cared about anyone here but you. Why would she care about me or any of the girls?" Black tears ruined her makeup and smudged the sides of her contorting face. "I don't know shit, I swear. I already told you I don't know shit," she wheezed.

I put the knife back in my boot and pushed her head up toward me. "Fine. Hear this out, though. If I ever find out you do know shit or

I do as much as suspect you're sniffing around for Beth or catch a glimpse of you near my room for any reason, you're dead. You hear me?"

She nodded, trembling, her eyes squeezing.

I yanked at her hair again. "Can't hear you."

"Yes! Yes, Dusty," she whimpered.

I let go of her. "Now be a good bitch and spread the word. Don't wanna run around shooting club whores now." I winked at her and smacked her ass. "It's bad for business."

She tripped over the porch as she darted away from me. The back of her hand was wiping her face as she got off the steps. Then she disappeared in the woods.

I eyed the guys around the bonfire. "Ginger!"

Skid's younger brother looked my way. I nodded at the woods. Without a word, he stood and marched to keep an eye on Serena.

From now on, all Beth's girls would be followed. No one breathed without my knowing about it. If the cunt found refuge at another chapter or a rival club, she'd start a war or at least try to set a hit on Cammie again. For that she'd need intel. Who would be a better snitch than her own whores?

If the brothers didn't find her tonight, I'd just sit and wait for her to make that mistake.

CHAPTER 17

DUSTY

"A little harsh on the girls?" Owl sat on my bed, his flashlight pen in hand.

I snapped my head over to him and held his stare. He was hovering over the line, and when he broke the stare, I knew he got it.

He lifted Cammie's lids one by one. "Just saying Beth turned her back on them, too. She controlled everything from within. Even the books."

"Is that how you're telling me you can't do your new job?"

"The whole system is a fucking mess. She didn't make it exactly accessible for anyone else to use it." He checked the IV and the monitor of the beeping machine next to the bed. "Anyway, I'm working backward from now. How far back do you want me to go?"

Trusting my own parents was a slip on my side. Trust itself was a deadly mistake that I wouldn't make twice. "Until the very beginning."

Owl's bushy brows hooked. "You're being a dick."

I watched Cammie's sleeping figure sprawled out on the bed, half-bruised, her arm in a cast. "Can you blame me?"

He just sighed and emptied her bag of piss.

"When is she going to wake up? This's taking way too fucking long. Do I need to take her to a fucking hospital?"

"When it comes to brain injuries we have no certainties. She was badly beaten. She needs time to heal."

I took off my boots and stretched beside her. The devious girl that barged into my life, changing it forever. The beautiful stranger that kidnapped me and stole my heart in the process.

"Get some sleep, Dusty. You're no good to her when you're exhausted and unable to think straight."

"You go to bed. I'll take care of her meds through the night."

He shook his head, sighing again. "Just do me a favor and don't go snorting powder on me now. There's no way up from there."

I tried to smile and failed. "Night, Doc."

As soon as he closed the door, I started the routine of moving her limbs and checking for bedsores. She had none so far. Owl assured me those didn't form until at least a week if not several. The idea alone of her lying like this for weeks made me wanna kill something.

I stroked her beautiful, long hair and kissed her forehead. "Please wake up, sweetheart. I love you so much. Don't know what I'd do without you."

CHAPTER 18

CAMERON

A loud beeping disturbed my sleep. It was too close, right in my ear, inside my brain. It wouldn't shut up.

My alarm didn't sound like that. Neither did Ashley's. Besides, she was never up before me. What the fuck was going on? Were we late to Professor Lahey's class?

A smell of alcohol wafted into my nostrils and had me instantly confused. Suspicious. It wasn't liquor alcohol; it was...sterilization. Our apartment was never clean enough to smell sterile.

I tried to open my eyes, but they were glued shut. My arms and legs defied me, too. I couldn't move any part of my body.

"When is she going to wake up? This's taking way too fucking long. Do I need to take her to a fucking hospital?" Dusty's rugged voice demanded desperately.

"When it comes to brain injuries we have no certainties. She was badly beaten. She needs time to heal," a softer, older voice responded.

Panic coursed over me. Brain injury? Badly beaten? Was I paralyzed?

Then the memories hit, their weight settling over me when I saw Ashley's body swimming in its own blood, when I realized what happened after. The pain, not something I'd ever forget. And the gunshot that followed. The trigger I squeezed.

I put all of my effort into moving my mouth, my fingertips, anything to make some kind of sound to alert the people around me that I was here. But I couldn't. My body refused to obey me. I was trapped in my own body, unable to control it.

"Please wake up, sweetheart. Don't know what I'd do without you." Dusty's voice came closer.

The panic spread under every inch of my skin but was quickly replaced by darkness I sank in once more.

CHAPTER 19

DUSTY

My phone buzzed persistently, waking me up out of a restless sleep to alert me it was time to give Cameron her meds. I yawned and checked the time. Three a.m. I must have been so exhausted that my body eventually gave in and dozed off while I curled up next to her.

I stretched my tired muscles and reached for the pack of brown ampules and a syringe on the nightstand. I narrowed my eyes at the pack to make sure it was the right one, but there were no syringes left. I scratched the back of my head, yawning again as I walked to the bathroom cabinet.

Quickly, I grabbed a syringe and opened the package with my teeth. Then I walked back into the bedroom and turned on the lamp. Kneeling beside the bed, I gently touched her uninjured arm. "Cammie, wake up. It's time for your meds."

Her silence had never failed to punch me in the gut.

"No?" A sad sigh seeped out of my chest. Why had I been so hopeful tonight, thinking she would wake up and answer me, wishing I'd hear her sexy rasp call my name? This was so fucked up. *I* was so fucked up.

"Okay, baby. Take your time. I'm not going anywhere." I broke the ampule and filled the syringe with the medicine. Then I emptied the air and pushed it in the IV.

After it was all done, and I cleaned up, I took one last look at Cammie and turned off the light.

"Dusty."

I jumped, and then froze, and then turned on my heels. Was I hallucinating in the dark? No. I'd recognize this rasp any place any time. She did sound like she'd smoked a pack of Marlboros last night, but it was still hers.

My old lady's rasp.

I switched on the lamp again, and she was looking at me.

"Cammie? Holy shit, you're awake. Thank fuck." Without a second thought, my mouth swooped down and crushed hers. "Owl! Get in here!"

She stared at me as if she didn't recognize me. Then she looked down the bed, noticing the cast and the IV. "Where am I?"

"In my room, sweetheart." I grinned. "Can't believe you're up. You've been sleeping for a week. OWL!"

"I think I might have to go back to sleep for a bit."

"No, no, no, no, Cammie. Cammie, baby, wake up. Just stay awake, Cameron!"

She didn't hear me and drifted back into the abyss that had been sucking her whole.

"FUCK!" I kicked a fucking chair as Owl dashed into the room in a wifebeater and jeans, barefoot.

He hurried to the monitor. "What happened?"

"She was up for like three seconds and then fell back into a fucking coma."

"Chill. It's totally normal."

"Normal? Don't fucking tell me this shit. You're a fucking doctor. Wake her up!"

He got a pin from his pocket. "Did she speak?"

I paced the room like a caged animal. "Yes."

"Good." Owl poked her on several places and used that pin on her feet and hands. Then he checked her with the fucking flashlight thing.

My hands clasped behind my head as he came to me. "Her vitals are great. Her nerves are fine. It's a good sign that she spoke. It means there's no brain damage. You just have to—"

"Fucking wait. Yeah, I got it!" I kicked something else and heard something smash, too enraged to notice what it was. "But I'm tired of waiting. I mean she was up, man, looking at me, speaking to me. What the fuck just happened?"

"You look like you're about to get an aneurism. That won't help when she's actually up. She needs you, Dusty…in your right fucking mind."

"Prez." Ginger came up to my door.

"What?" I asked, my eyes on Cammie.

"Skid and Big Gun are back with the drivers."

Their timing couldn't be better. I hoped those fucking drivers didn't want to talk. I looked at Owl. "Stay here. Don't let her out of your sight till I get back."

CHAPTER 20

DUSTY

We were four people in the Boiler. Two had no choice but to be here. Jared, the driver who took Beth to Detroit, was pissing himself in a corner. Shane something, the other driver who wouldn't tell me yet where he'd taken her after she left Wrench's place, was shaking in fear in another corner.

"Please stop." The begging was followed by another scream and plea for mercy as Big Gun cut into that Jared fuck.

Now it was my turn to get Shane to speak and blow out some steam in the process. I hit his head with pry bars, knocking him to the ground in no time. "I won't ask you again." I threw the tool and grabbed my knife from my boot. "Where the fuck did you drop her?"

"In the middle of nowhere," he sniffled. "I already told you. I swear."

I dragged my knife down the man's arm. Fresh blood bloomed on his flesh under the blade before spilling down. "And where exactly is that middle of nowhere?"

"Kentucky," he groaned. "I dropped her on the road. There were no other cars. No people. Nothing. I drove away for half a mile, and she was still standing there."

We didn't have chapters in Kentucky. She knew leaving her there would be a dead end for me to follow. Fuck.

I punched the guy until I smashed his face and his blood smeared mine. Even if I killed him, my rage wouldn't go away.

"Prez…" Big Gun stopped my fist in midair, the piece of shit under me choking on his breath.

I straightened and nodded at my Enforcer.

Big Gun sliced his knife across the throat of the driver, silencing him forever.

CHAPTER 21

CAMERON

I opened my eyes to a light spilling through a corner in the room, my vision blurry. It took a few minutes for the place to come into focus. I was cold, my head hazy, my arm in a cast, the other hooked up to an IV and the machine that kept beeping in my head. A huge, black t-shirt covered me mid thighs, its smell familiar. I gave myself a moment to get my bearings then sat up.

Shit. Pain radiated so hard through my broken body I cried. Why did I hurt all over like I'd been hit by a fucking truck?

I pushed myself upright and breathed deeply to fight back the waves of nausea rolling over me. "Fuck." My breaths caught for a few seconds. Gritting my teeth, I swung my legs to dangle over the side of the bed, reaching out to the IV pole beside my bed.

Sounds of running water came from the lit corner in the room. I assumed it was a bathroom, and someone was taking a shower. I tried to recall the previous day's events, but my memory was foggy as hell. Where was I? What was I doing here? My pulse raced as images of broken glass and blood flashed in my head. The last thing I remembered clearly was a sound of a gunshot.

My vagina throbbed with pain, and I realized I had to use the bathroom. I took a deep breath and reached my feet down to touch the cold tiles. Then I held on to the IV pole and walked slowly out of the bed.

"Cammie!" Dusty exclaimed with a hint of panic. I glanced up to see him striding from the bathroom toward me, arms extended, half-naked, nothing but a towel wrapped around his waist, water dripping from his long hair. "You gotta stop doing this shit to me." A huge grin stretched his mouth. "You up for real this time?"

"What?" I lost my footing and stumbled toward the floor. His strong arms caught me before impact.

"What the fuck you think you're doing?" he growled as he placed me back on the edge of the bed.

A hulking figure came through the bedroom door, his eyes down, his shoulders slumped. He held what looked like a saline bag. Dusty yelled at the old man, something about not leaving me alone.

The guy looked at the two of us. "I was getting a new one. Looks like we don't need it anymore." He turned on the lights and came closer. Gray peppered his hair and trimmed beard. Full sleeves and neck tattoos. Mostly skulls and roses. He was definitely a Night Skull.

My head snapped at Dusty. Immediately, I regretted the nausea caused by the sudden move. "Am I in Rosewood?"

He took a deep breath and just nodded. I looked around, confirming it was indeed Dusty's room.

The older Skull's blue eyes shone at me. "It's okay. Don't worry. You're safe and finally up after eight days in a coma. Let's check on you. Can you tell me your name?"

My eyes narrowed at him. My mind struggled to grasp what was really happening here. Why the hell was I in Rosewood, the place I swore never to come back to since it killed my sister and almost took my own life? And how long had I been down here…sleeping? "Cameron Delaney. What's yours?"

He chuckled. "Owl or Doc. The club's on call doctor." He pulled out a pen light and looked into my eyes, and then listened to my heartbeat for a few seconds. "Welcome back, Cameron." The bed sank beside me as he sat. He pulled my good hand out, pressing against it as he asked me to press back.

After I did, and he confirmed to Dusty that my uninjured arm was good, the doctor asked me to smile.

"Smile? Why would I smile for you?"

He chuckled again. "Just to make sure your facial muscles are working."

I raised a brow and flashed him a quick smile. My jaws and lips hurt like hell. Then Owl's hands were all over me, and Dusty kept asking if I was all right with every part of my body the doctor checked.

"Well, shit. You look pretty good to me. The question is how do you feel, princess?" Owl asked.

"Feel?" I had no idea how I felt. My memory was fucked up. Everything seemed…dry. Stilted. On hold. "I feel like I wanna pee. Really need to use the bathroom."

I tried to stand again, but Dusty's wet body pressed against me. "You don't need to get out of bed for that, sweetheart." He pointed down to a bag attached to me. One filled with yellow liquid that could only be one thing.

Heat snuck up to my cheeks in embarrassment. I'd been pissing myself in front of my boyfriend for God knew how long. "Shit."

"It's okay, baby. There's nothing to be embarrassed about. You've been out for eight fucking days. The most stressful, fucked up days of my life. Now that you're up, I wouldn't care if you took a dump right here, not just piss in a bag."

I scrutinized Dusty's face. His excitement was beyond my conception. I got that he was relieved I was awake; I was out for so long after what I, in spite of not remembering its details, was sure was a day from hell. But I was also sure he'd had more fucked up days— like the ones he had in my bunker. And my being in Rosewood was nothing to be happy about.

"I'm not gonna go in front of you." My gaze shifted to Owl. "Or you. Take the catheter out."

"Slow down, princess. I know these things are a pain in the crotch, but let's keep it till we're sure you can move fully on your own. You still need your rest," Owl said.

"You said I was fine, and I was just about to leave the bed by *myself*."

"But you almost fell down." Dusty squatted and held my arms. "Cammie, please. Just till morning. Give your ol'man some peace of mind."

Princess. Ol'man. Rosewood. What the fuck was I doing here?

I stared at Dusty. His care and concern fell empty on me for the first time ever. Was I still mad at him for Samuel? Memories flashed in my head, trimmed. Yeah, we broke up over it, but it left me devastated. I knew I was still in love with him, but I didn't quite *feel* it. "Fine. Just till morning. But I still need to go in the privacy of a bathroom."

He sighed, yielding. "Okay, let's get you on your feet. Just put one arm around me and the other one around Owl, and we'll get you up real nice and slow."

I winced in pain as they pulled me up. A grunt forced itself out of my mouth as I engaged my abdomen and thigh muscles. I stood on my feet, a little wobbly, but I stayed upright.

The pain was too much, yet what really caught my attention was that when I felt the warmth of Dusty on my right, I didn't feel a chill run along my skin like always.

This wasn't because I was angry. Anger didn't do that. I was numb. Impervious to…feelings.

I put one foot in front of the other, and after several steps, I removed my arms from around their shoulders. Dusty kept his warm hand on the small of my back as I continued forward, refusing to let go until I was in the bathroom.

He smiled. "I'm right outside if you need anything. And I mean anything."

"Thanks." I was about to close the door, but then I turned my head back to him. "Actually, can you call Ash, tell her I'm all right? She must be worried sick."

CHAPTER 22

CAMERON

"Ash?" The look on Dusty's face contracted the muscles around my heart.

Groggy, I shifted on my feet, holding tight to the pole. "Yes. I had the worst dream in my coma, and now I'm worried sick. She must be worried too. Have you heard from her?"

He glanced sideways in Owl's direction, and then he looked back at me. "Cammie, what's the last thing you remember?"

"A gu…" I was about to tell him about the gunshot, but I swallowed my words short. I didn't want to let him know about the fuzzy memory, especially when he was looking at me like I was a crazy person. He'd think I was suffering from amnesia, and he'd make me stay in bed much longer.

And…there was this strange emotion I couldn't identify that snuck up on me every time I was focused on remembering exactly what happened to me. Something I wasn't ready to deal with right now.

"Cammie?" he repeated.

"I really need to pee." I slammed the door shut.

A mirror greeted me, condensation from Dusty's shower blurring the glass. I wiped it and came face to face with myself.

Startled for a minute at the bruises, puffy eyes and cuts on my lips, I gripped the edge of the sink so I wouldn't collapse. The IV pricked my hand as I examined my nose. It was definitely broken like my arm. My good hand moved slowly over my body, stopping once at my abdomen and again on my back. These two areas hurt and burned the most.

I wanted to take off the t-shirt to take a look at my back and see if I had new scars, but my hand flew to my head as I sat on the toilet, about to pass out from the sudden pain. Throbbing. Pounding. Exploding heat frying my brain. "Fuck!"

"Baby, you all right?" Dusty's knock felt like a thousand drums banging at once.

"I'm fine," I lied.

"You sure?"

My eyes shot up. "If I need anything, I'll call for you. Can you please give me some fucking privacy?"

He swore, his steps moving away from the door.

An angry sob ripped out of my chest as memories flooded through me; the events of the attack crammed in my mind.

Pain.

Fear.

Blood.

Broken glass.

Gunshot.

The pain inflicted by the punches and smashes of a huge man in a mask. The paralyzing fear of thinking I was going to be raped and murdered. By someone who was supposed to be protecting me. A man I knew but couldn't remember his face.

Blood was everywhere. I crawled away on broken glass, running for my life, my skin tearing to shreds. Horror after horror until he was on top of me.

And then…

Bang.

"I killed him," I muttered to myself, staring at my hands. Then my eyes trailed to my arms, chest, and stomach, seeing the blood that had once covered them from head to toe. "*I pulled the trigger. I fucking killed him!*"

"Cammie, I'm coming in!" Dusty yelled through the door and burst in, looking beyond worried. He was now wearing jeans, his chest bare yet dry. His eyes softened when he saw me, and he gently pulled me into his arms.

"*I killed him.*" It was more of a question than a statement. I needed a confirmation that I had murdered a person, not that I felt one bit of regret. I just needed to know if I had crossed that one line and took a life with my own hands.

"This was not your fault. None of this is your fault." He squeezed me a little tighter. "Rush deserved to die."

Rush.

That was the man in the mask.

Suddenly, I could see his face. His green eyes that looked like Dusty's. The flashes raced through my consciousness, planting a deep ball of misery in my gut.

My head whipped up. "He was your real father. Beth. She was behind it all. She set him on me because she wanted you to stay

President. They did this together." I told him everything I recalled about that night. I'd never seen Dusty cry. His eyes shone with tears, yet mine were cement dry. I was reciting the horrors that I'd gone through, and while a man as rough as Dusty was being deeply affected by my words, I felt nothing.

"It's okay, baby. I know. I'm so sorry. *I'm so sorry!*" He framed my head with his hands. "You're safe now, here with me. I'd never let anything hurt you again."

Safe?

That word should be removed from our dictionary. The President of the Night Skulls and his *ol'lady*. I snorted in my head.

He pressed me back to his chest. "Baby, there's something I need to tell you."

"There's more to that horrible day than I recall, isn't it?" I asked, his heartbeat thumping in my ear.

"It's…"

He didn't need to say it. It was all coming back to me, slicing at my heart, darkening my soul. I could see it in my head. The pool of blood. The hole in her head. "It wasn't really a dream."

"No, baby. The son of a bitch put a bullet in Ash's head."

I nodded. I only fucking nodded.

It was as if he was talking about someone I never cared about. Never considered as my little sister. Why the hell wasn't I crying? Why wasn't I pushing him off me and screaming in his face?

There was this big fucking numb darkness crawling, spreading to every corner of my heart, wrapping around my soul so tightly, turning every shred of emotion inside me into…nothing.

"Cammie? Did you hear me, baby?"

He, too, was wondering why I wasn't reacting as I should have been. Why I was dead inside.

"Yes." I lifted my head off his chest. "Where is Beth?"

"Beth will get what she deserves. Don't worry about her or anything else. All we need to do now is get you better."

"Is she here? We need to ask her what Rush meant when he said you wouldn't kill him."

"What exactly did he say?"

"He said there was a lot I didn't know, and you couldn't kill him because you wouldn't make the same mistake twice. He made sure of it." I stared at him. "Beth must have plotted something with him, a leverage of sorts that would stop you from killing him. We need to question her and make her talk."

"I will, baby. I'll take care of it."

"Bring her now. Where is she?"

Here came that stare again. "She ran away. But don't worry. I'll find her, and you will have your revenge."

My revenge was to see that motherfucking bitch drowning in her own blood. "I don't think you can give me that. She's your mother after all."

"Not anymore." Rage pulsed off his body. His fists clenched and unclenched. An unfamiliar fire blazed in his eyes. Not the kind of anger I was used to from him. It was…morbid and sad. Deep. "There's something else you need to know."

"What?"

"You were…" he muttered under his breath, his voice thick with that same sad fury. "The assault… We lost our baby."

My mind took some time to register what he'd just said, yet something faster flicked inside me. Instinct, I guessed. "I was pregnant?"

He nodded, his eyes reddening. "Owl, Doc, estimated you were about two or three weeks."

I blinked as tears burned my eyes. But they wouldn't fall. I wouldn't let them fall.

The pain in my abdomen and vagina was accounted for now. I was beaten and raped until I had a miscarriage. My hand touched my stomach. Instantly, I felt emptier than I already was.

Dusty embraced me and showered my head with little, warm, quick kisses, telling me it was okay to cry and take my time to grieve.

I pulled away fast. "Why would I do that? It's best that we lost it."

He stared at me like I'd just backstabbed him. "What?"

"You heard me. You couldn't be possibly thinking about having children."

"A year ago, maybe. But after I met you, everything has changed. You drive me crazy I forget to pull out, still I rarely use protection with you. Don't you remember how I was so fucking determined to put a baby in your belly the stupid night you broke up with me? To maybe leave something from me inside you that will bring you back to me? I want everything with you, Cameron."

"That's not what I meant. Look around you, Dusty. Look at yourself. What I'm saying is that the world doesn't need any more Night Skulls' offspring."

His eyes narrowed at me. It seemed that I'd hurt him deep. "I know you're in a fucking dark place right now, and you don't mean any of the shit you're saying. But you don't have to be a dick."

I just looked at him.

He shut the door, and then cupped my face in his hands, his eyes soft again. "Baby, once I find Beth and close this page for good, we'll go away like you always wanted," he whispered. "We'll start a family far away from all this shit where you can be safe and happy." His lips touched mine gently. "I love you, Cammie."

I didn't return his kiss. "What do you mean we'll go away?"

"I'll leave the Night Skulls. Will close the chapter if I have to," he whispered again. "Fuck, I'd already left that night. That's what I came to tell you then." He kept going on and on, making promises of a better life. Promises a guy like him could never keep.

"Look what your trying to leave got us. You will do no such thing again," I interrupted, keeping my voice low. Obviously, he didn't want anybody to hear about his plans.

"No, baby. We have to get out of here. You were right about this place. And after what happened, we have to—"

"I was wrong. You should have never left. I should have never asked you to do so. We're living here. It's where you belong. It's where I belong now."

A grimace distorted his face. His eyes pierced into me. "Cammie—"

"I'm not going anywhere. We're running this *club*. Together."

CHAPTER 23

DUSTY

Who would have ever thought Cameron Delaney would say she wanted to live in Rosewood with the Night Skulls and run the fucking place?

I chuckled at the thought, not paying much attention to how serious she looked when she said that shit. She was still in shock. She hadn't shed a fucking tear. Her head was a fucked up mess, and she needed time to get it together and think straight again.

To open up again.

I watched Cammie in her sleep after Owl gave her enough painkillers to knock her out for what was left of the night and the next morning. Even with all the bruises, she still looked like an angel.

A bruised angel. That was exactly what she was right now. It was hard to imagine someone that had gone through as much as she had and not become lost and confused like she was.

My gaze trailed back and forth to her closed eyelids, her lips and her chest. She stirred, moaning a little, the covers slid off and her t-shirt rode up to her hips.

Fuck. Because of the catheter, she wasn't wearing panties. I could see her sweet pussy, and, instantly, my cock ached. Well, I had a semi-erection all the time I was watching her, and now I was wishing my cock was a fucking catheter. How fucked up and pathetic was that?

"I need you, Cammie. I miss you so much, baby. That shit talk wasn't exactly what I had in mind when you finally woke up. I imagined it'd have been a lot nicer. Like we'd have both cried in each other's arms, and then I'd have told you I was here for you, ready to do anything to protect you and make you happy again. Then I'd have showed you how much I missed and loved you, groveling and begging for your forgiveness, hoping you would forgive me because you still loved me." I ran the back of my fingers across her cheek, using all my willpower not to feel her up. I didn't want to wake her, and I didn't know how she would react after what that piece of shit did to her.

A kiss won't hurt though. I pressed my lips against hers as softly as I could, but then I grew greedy. Hungry. I should have dragged myself out of the room before I touched her because now I couldn't stop.

My hands roamed over her body. I filled my palms with her tits, my nose breathing her skin in. Even in her sleep, her nipples hardened under my touch. My cock twitched painfully, so I freed my erection and gave myself a stroke or two.

I hadn't gotten my dick wet in weeks. Since the breakup I fucked nothing but my fist, thinking about my beautiful Cammie and the day she'd be bouncing on my cock again, drenching me with her sweet cum.

My tongue darted to lick my lips as my stare landed on her naked pussy. My fingers traced the pink flesh that glistened in response. Fuck. I spread her legs apart for a better view, and my fist moved faster around my shaft, wishing she'd wake up to see how much I wanted her, how much power she had over me. How helpless I was in front of her beauty that I couldn't bridle my desire for her and was fucking myself in her sleep, watching her like a sick creep.

"Sorry, baby, but I just can't see your naked, wet pussy and not come." As if she heard me, a drop of her juice trickled out begging me to be licked. Stroking myself harder, I lapped my tongue over her, consuming every drop until I wiped her clean and then wet her all over again with my own cum.

As I came down from that, I was about to get a washcloth and clean my mess, but the sight of my cum on her pussy was so pretty I didn't want it gone. Instead, I slowly, intently, pushed it all inside her where it belonged.

When I was done, I leaned in for a whisper. "When you're healed, sweetheart, I'll come inside you every day until you carry my baby again. Don't worry. There is nothing in the world that would dare come near you again. I won't allow it, I promise."

The sun was about to rise when I left the room and reached the porch. The wind blew pretty bad and refused to let me light my cigarette. Yeah, I smoked. I needed something to take off the edge but wanted to stay alert at the same time. Apart from the occasional joint, I didn't do any drugs.

Don't worry, Owl. I won't go snorting my own shit. I'm gonna fuck up my lungs instead.

The wind rumbled through the trees, sending waves of debris all over the place. I took a couple of steps toward the door to shield the flame, and I was glad I fucking did.

A loud noise boomed behind me. I spun to see that a huge chunk from the roof flew and tumbled right where I was standing. Fuck.

Carefully, I tilted my head up, the wind making cheesy horror movie sounds. I backed the hell up as another chunk came flying off.

I'd only been living here for a few months since last year. When was the last time Roar did any work on this old estate?

Ginger staggered through the door, narrowing stoned as fuck, sleepy eyes at the rubble, wild red curls dangling down his head. "You all right, Prez?"

I threw away my cigarette. "It missed me by a fucking inch, thank you for asking. We gotta repair this shit...right fucking now."

His little nose scrunched up. "Now, Prez? It's barely even morning."

I didn't give a shit. What if Cammie decided to take a walk or it fucking rained and water went through the ceiling of the bedroom? "Yeah. Now."

He dropped his gaze and mumbled, "Okay. I'll go wake some brothers."

A Harley roar mixed with the wind in the background. Skid cruised through the gates as his little brother yelled for the boys.

Skid stowed the bike and reached me, broody as fuck. "What happened here?"

I offered him a cigarette and tried to light another one myself. "What happened to *you*?"

A sigh burst out of his chest as he shielded the wind away with his cut. "I need a favor."

The harsh smoke filled our lungs. "Yeah?"

"My kid. Can I let him crash here for a couple of weeks?"

I never liked the idea of a little child hanging around here. It's one of my unspoken rules. I, of all people, knew what this place could do to an innocent boy. Skid knew about the rule. He'd have never asked if something wasn't seriously wrong. If one of the brothers needed help with his family, I'd never say no.

"Sure," I said. "What happened to Molly?"

He sucked in a deep breath off the cigarette and blew it fast. "Using again."

"Shit."

"Yeah. Same old Molly." His gaze drifted off. "I should put a bullet in her head and get all her shit over with."

I snorted.

He glared at me. "You don't fucking believe I'd do that one day, do ya?"

"Not in a million years. She got you by the pussy."

He flicked the cigarette away, rolling his eyes. "Thanks for letting my kid stay here, Prez. He'll be out in a week or two…once she sobers the fuck up."

"Take as much time as you need. Just keep him out of trouble. And don't go anywhere. We have a roof to repair."

CHAPTER 24

CAMERON

I bolted upright in Dusty's bed, covered in sweat. Excessive hammering had snatched me out of a nightmare. Then pain shot down every part of my body, a constant reminder my own life was a nightmare itself.

Running a hand through my mess of a hair, I squinted at the dark orange sun flaring through the windows. How long had I been sleeping? And what the hell was that continuous hammering?

My heart leapt at the door opening without a warning. Then Owl stepped inside.

I grimaced. "You enter Dusty's room without even knocking?"

He raised his hands up to his chest. "Sorry, princess. Thought you were sleeping. Came to wake you up for your pain meds and to give you some food."

The tension building in my shoulders eased a bit. "I don't think I need more of those. I feel better." That wasn't a lie; the pain was a lot, but it was the only thing I could feel now. I didn't want that taken away as well. I was starving, though.

He picked up a tray off the floor and kicked the door shut. "Oh, yes you will. When the ones I gave you wear off in a few minutes." He set the tray on my legs and went through the medication bottles on the nightstand.

As if on cue, the wounds on my back and legs screamed at me. My shoulders slumped in surrender.

He pushed something through my IV. "Don't worry. I'm not giving you anything too strong. I know how it is to get hung up on these little bitches."

"What?"

He sat on the edge of the bed, full of energy and…grace. Even though he was in his late forties, maybe even early fifties, he moved and was built like a twenty year old. "Never mind. Let's get some protein in there."

He uncovered one of the two plates on the tray, and I saw a huge piece of grilled steak and a bowl of mashed potatoes. The other plate had a grilled, boneless chicken breast and jasmine rice. "Didn't know what you preferred so I made both chicken and steak."

I stared at the tray, the mouthwatering smell of the food filling my nostrils. "You made these?"

"Yup."

"Thank you." I was about to grab a fork, but I hesitated for a moment.

"I'll take a piece of everything if it eases your mind."

I laughed under my breath, not meeting his eyes. "I didn't mean…"

"It's all right, princess. I wouldn't blame you if you did."

"Did Dusty tell you to cook for me?"

He nodded. "Wouldn't let any of the girls do it. Actually, since you've gotten in Rosewood, no one is allowed up here alone but me and him."

I blinked at the plates. "Does that mean I'm in danger?"

"Just because the Skulls aren't fond of you at the moment doesn't mean you're in danger.

But he has every right to protect you. Even if he has to be a fucking dick about it. Better safe than sorry."

"Well, my feelings for the Night Skulls are more than mutual." I glanced back at him. "What about you?"

"What about me?"

"He trusts you enough to let you take care of me. Does that mean you don't hate me?"

A smirk curved up the corner of his lips. "I think it just means he trusts me enough to let me take care of his old lady while he's gone."

Fair enough. Why would any Night Skull, even a composed, not so obnoxious doctor, not hate me? I kidnapped their current president, was the reason their former president wound up dead, and killed their VP with my own hands. They didn't care if they were nasty villains who hurt and killed innocent people for their own gain because that was what the Skulls were. Nasty fucking villains. They didn't give a shit "Where's Dusty?"

"If he wanted to tell you, he would have." He picked up a fork and gave it to me. "Now eat. Or do you want me to cut your food and feed you like a baby?"

I cocked a brow. It looked like I formed an opinion about him too quickly. He was obnoxious like the rest. "Maybe I do."

He got off the bed. "Fuck that. I'm not gonna do this shit. I'm not a babysitter."

My arms folded across my chest, my brow still shot high. "Yes, you will because I won't eat any other way. You think *Prez* will be pleased to know you failed to get his ol'lady to eat?"

A murderous glare wrinkled the corners around his eyes, yet a smile tugged at his lips. "Princess has claws."

"More sharp than you think, or don't you remember how I met your Prez in the first place?"

He sat next to me again and started cutting the steak, perfect juice streaming out of it. "I like you a little better now."

I rolled my eyes. A little pressure down my abdomen reminded me I had to pee. "Before I eat, I really need you to take that catheter off me. It's really embarrassing to go like this."

He laughed. "That I can't do without Dusty in the room. He might still trust me but not that much."

"Seriously?"

"Dead serious. He'll literally kill me for it."

My lips twisted as I tried to hold it; I wasn't gonna pee while he was a few inches away. "Okay, you don't have to cut my food. I was messing with you."

A smile touched his bright blue eyes before his lips. "I know, and I don't mind. I miss the feeling."

I narrowed my gaze at him. "You have children?"

His smile vanished. By the look on his face, I'd say I'd triggered an awful memory. "If I show you how to remove the catheter, can you do it yourself?"

Had I crossed a line or something? "Sure." I dismissed the topic without a second thought. Everyone was entitled to their secrets. Especially if they were too dark to tell.

CHAPTER 25

CAMERON

Whoever invented catheters was a sadist. It took one to know one.

After a normal, yet rather painful pee on the toilet, I took a long look at myself in the bathroom mirror. The swelling had been a little better, and it felt good to stand freely without needles or poles or something stuffed in my vagina; once I ate, Owl was convinced I didn't need the IV anymore.

However, I was still numb on the inside as if I'd never had a heart to break or a soul to hurt. That big fat nothing had dug inside me way so deeply I could barely recognize myself.

I took off Dusty's t-shirt to take a shower. The first view of the scars on my back made me flinch. Then I stared at them for minutes. The evidence of the ugliness the Night Skulls imposed on me.

They were my curse, and they made sure I'd never forget that.

Little did they know they weren't scaring me away when they scarred me for life. They were forging me into one of them instead. Now the time had come to show them I was the curse of their lives, too. And just like they did, I'd make sure they never forgot.

I showered, brushed my teeth, put on clean t-shirt and sweatpants of Dusty's, and combed my wet hair. Then I decided to go outside.

Owl helped me down the stairs, the nonstop hammering louder with every step. I'd never seen inside the house before. The only part of Rosewood I saw, beside Dusty's room, was a bushy, unattended garden— where I was tied to a fucking tree—and a dried out pool.

Despite its serious need of maintenance and cleaning, downstairs was a vast open hall that served all purposes. A kitchen on the right. A bar right across from it. A dartboard on the wall and an air hockey table inches away beneath it. A sitting area with a TV and leather couches on the left. It was also a place to get blowjobs and fuck while everybody watched.

The couple doing it on one of the couches and the guy pushing a blonde's head down his cock didn't stop when I came down. Everything else did, though. The laughter. The chatter. The drinking. The cooking. The room fell in silence, except for the sex sounds and the stupid hammering.

Suddenly, it was my last day at school all over again. All eyes were on me, and not a single stare was friendly. They were looking at me as if I murdered someone. Only this time, it was true.

I did murder Rush.

From what I saw in their eyes, it didn't matter Rush killed my best friend and was halfway into raping me. Why I pulled the trigger didn't mean anything to them. All that mattered was that I killed the Night Skulls' VP.

I took a deep breath and focused my gaze on Owl. "Are you fixing something outside?"

"It got a little windy early this morning, and the roof gave." He gestured at the dingy walls. "It's an old house."

I noticed the scaffolding through the open front door. "I should take a look at that."

Loud, mocking laughs filled the air.

On any given day, I'd have felt self-conscious or angry about men thinking I wasn't good enough to do *man's work* even when I was getting a degree for it. I'd have thought of something smart to say, a snide comment to shove down those mansplaining throats.

Not today.

That big fat nothing swallowing me came in handy, and I just didn't care. Not the *push your feelings aside because they were not worth it* kind of didn't care. I just didn't. The bobbing Adam's apples, ugly teeth, smelly breaths and awful faces looking at me like I was a silly little girl didn't mean anything at all.

It was liberating.

"Zip it. Prez won't be pleased to know you've been laughing at his old lady," Owl said, giving everyone around a menacing stare.

A guy with a bandana on his head scratched his balls. "Old lady my ass. Isn't she the one behind all the shenanigans that's fucking up this place?"

"A bad luck pussy is what she is," another guy said, squashing a beer can with one fist. "Every man that tries to touch it winds up taken, beaten or dead."

Another roar of laughter erupted.

"You wanna tell Prez that to his face?" Owl asked, and the laughter was chopped off. "Yeah. Now you shut up."

"Can I get you anything, darling?" A woman in the kitchen said. Her hair was raven black. She wore red lipstick and black eyeliner. A red tank top showed her lace bra and half of her inflated boobs. She had a full sleeve and more tattoos on her back and the top of her chest. "A beer?"

Her grin was forced, fake like her boobs. Suck-up? I couldn't decide right away. Maybe it was a professional habit. I knew a flight attendant once. She had this huge grin on her face the whole time even when she was off duty. I doubted this woman was a flight attendant, though. She probably tended bars or…serviced men. According to Dusty, these were the common professions here. No doubt the men laughed when I offered to take a look at the roof. They'd probably never met a female engineer before.

Well, an engineering student… Damn. I was a few months away from getting my degree. Now look at me.

My eyes wandered around the place. Yeah. I could use a drink. "I'd appreciate a Cosmo."

She stopped short at the counter, cocking her hip out and putting her hand on it, a bitch stare on her face. Then she rolled her eyes at Owl.

"Don't just stand there. Go make that shit," he ordered.

The woman gave me another bitch stare. This time, she raked me from head to toe and made sure I saw her do so. "She's not making it easy, you know?"

"The Cosmo, Candy."

She stalked to the cabinets, mumbling a few swears, as he ushered me to the bar.

"What did I do now?" I winced as I stretched to sit on the cherry wood stool. The pain killers were mellow as he said. I definitely needed something stronger.

"Ordering pink shit only an uptight bitch that doesn't belong here would drink."

"I see."

"Like I said, princess, nobody likes you around here. It will be a tough stay."

I smirked. "Did Dusty tell you to tell me that?"

His blue eyes darkened as he glared at me. "No."

My drink arrived. Candy almost threw it in my face when she put it down.

Owl shifted his glare at her, and she spun on her heels and dwindled in the kitchen. "Seriously now, when are you leaving?"

The expression on his face harbored on concern. The sincere kind. Too good to believe. "Why? Am I in danger here?" I stifled a snort.

"I told you before. You're Prez's old lady. No Night Skull would dare touch you." He leaned forward and met my stare. "But I think you're smart enough to understand that it's not the people here that pose a threat to you."

I moved my finger around the rim of the glass, looking through the froth, deciding not to drink. Candy might have spat in it. "Thank you for your concern, Owl. But I'm not going anywhere. This is home now."

The familiar roar of Dusty's Harley burst outside. Then he padded to the house, carrying a duffle bag. As soon as he spotted me, he smiled and hurried toward me.

He dropped the bag on the floor and practically pushed Owl aside to wrap me in his embrace. Then he gave me a kiss, one that used to melt my panties. "You're out of bed already?" His glanced turned to Owl. "Can she do that?"

The doctor nodded. "She's clear. For *everything*. She only needs to take her painkillers and antibiotics on time, and we're good."

Dusty's smile grew. "You heard that, sweetheart?"

"Yeah." I tried to pull away from him, but his arms were too tight around my waist.

"Where do you think you're going? I'm never gonna take my hands off you all night," he whispered in my ear.

Fuck. Did he really expect sex? Tonight? Putting all emotional and psychological damage aside after yet another sexual assault I had to endure, what about the actual physical concerns? My arm was in a fucking cast. My back was a mesh. My hips made audible sounds while I walked. I wouldn't even start about my vagina.

His eyes trailed on me. Then his brows hitched. "You fucking took off her catheter?"

Owl gave me a "what did I tell you?" look. "No, Dusty. She did. I only showed her a DIY video."

Dusty grunted as he noticed the Cosmo. "I see you met Candy. Anyone else?"

I didn't exactly favor Dusty's overprotectiveness, but I enjoyed it in this instant. It was a pain in the ass but warm at the same time.

I needed warm. *I guess.*

"Two charming Skulls over there. What are their names again, Owl?" I asked.

"Chain, the dude with the bandana, and Serial, the short guy," he answered.

"Chain and Serial," I repeated.

Dusty shot a murderous stare in the direction of the couches. "How's everybody treating you, baby?" He raised his voice.

"Like I said, they're very charming and considerate. Especially when I wanted to take a look at the roof. They were thrilled I offered but insisted it was such an easy job for an engineer like myself to bother with, and I should just chill and rest while they took care of everything." I twisted to see the looks on the men's faces. Their sweaty, blanching expressions made me smile for the first time since the attack. Precious. "Right boys?"

The two Skulls quickly nodded in unison.

I pointed at the kitchen. "And sweet Candy here didn't bat an eye when she offered me a beer, and I told her I only liked uptight bitch drinks. She laughed at my joke and made me a Cosmo. She even said she'd be delighted to make me one herself every night."

Dusty directed his lethal gaze at her, cocking a brow. "Every night?"

She trembled. "Sure, Prez."

He gave her a smile with no teeth. "Fucking awesome. I hope you don't miss one."

The menace in his voice sent a chill down *my* spine. I wondered what it did to her.

"I won't," she barely whispered, tears frozen in her eyes.

"I know you wouldn't." Dusty stroked my face, undressing me with his eyes. "Chain, Serial, go stand on that roof. Don't come down until I tell you to." He didn't take his gaze off me, studying my expression as he spoke.

There was some stirring. Someone cleared his throat, and Serial asked, "What?"

Yeah, what?

"You heard me, motherfuckers!" He was yelling, but his beautiful eyes were sparkling even brighter than usual at me. *I got you, sweetheart*, they said. *As long as I'm here, no one would hurt you, not even with a word. Whoever dared cross you would suffer. Don't worry, sweetheart. You're safe now.*

I dragged my gaze away from him and looked behind me. Slowly, the two men rose and ambled through the gloomy silence of this room and went through the front door.

CHAPTER 26

CAMERON

"Why did you do that to the men?" I tried to tie my hair up with one hand and failed miserably.

Dusty locked the bedroom door and laid the duffle bag on the bed. The hammering had finally stopped. "They were mean to you."

"I never said that."

"You said they were *charming and considerate*. You thought I wouldn't pick that up?" He flashed me a knowing grin. "No one dares to be mean to you and gets away with it. They're lucky they're still alive."

"You'd kill someone for just that?" I wasn't shocked or appalled. The rules were different in the MC world. I was just curious.

He frowned. "I know you don't like it, but yes, I would."

That sounded more appealing than it'd have ever had. I laughed at myself, at how naive I'd been before, how good and fucking self-righteous I'd been, breaking up with Dusty for beating the shit out of a bastard that was groping me, feeling so bad about Dusty almost killing him.

My gaze drifted away with the darkness falling outside the window. His big hands landed on my waist. His reflection appeared in the window as he planted a kiss on my neck. "Here, at least. It's the only language they understand," he added. "But when we're out, I promise I'll never hurt anyone again. Like you always wanted."

I took his hands off me and backed away from the window.

He sighed. "You have every right to stay mad at me. I'm sorry for what I did to your classmate. It won't ever happen again."

"I'm not mad at you, and I don't care about any of that. I don't even mind you killing anyone anymore. Some people deserved to die. *It's a necessity.*"

A deep line appeared between his brows as I repeated what he once told me. "No, baby. I was wrong, and I'm sorry. Everything you said was true. That's what I came to say that night, hoping you'd forgive me."

"Why the hell aren't you listening?"

"Because it's not you who are talking right now. It's this place. It's what it does to you, changes you from the inside out." He put his palms on either side of my face. "I swear if it was safe to send you somewhere else until I get Beth, I would. But Rosewood is the only place where I can really protect you."

I looked him directly in the eyes. "I already told you I'm not getting out of here. Not before or after we capture the bitch."

"Cammie...this is getting ridiculous."

I shrugged, too tired to argue. I found a chair and sat—I wasn't going to sit on the bed and give him any signals I was ready for whatever he had in mind for tonight. "Well, I'm sorry if you don't like the new me or the way I think, but I've changed, Dusty. A lot. Everything has changed."

He sat on the edge of the bed next to his duffle bag, facing me. "What are you telling me?"

"Cameron Delaney has blood on her hands. A murderer that doesn't belong to the outside world anymore. I am a Night Skull now whether you like it or not."

"You're shitting me right now."

"No. I'm embracing my destiny. There's no point in resisting."

"Cammie—"

"I've made up my mind and not gonna change it. You're just gonna have to deal with it."

CHAPTER 27

DUSTY

Deal with it my ass.

But if that was her game, I'd play. Patiently. As long as it took to put some fucking sense back into her head. She was too fucking stubborn. Any more pushing on my side would backfire. She had to change her mind on her own.

She will. A few more days in here, watching for herself what exactly meant to be a Night Skull, and she'd be begging me to leave.

"Have you appointed another VP yet?" she asked, deep in thought, not even looking at me.

Knowing Cameron, I knew exactly what she was going for with this. There was no way in fucking hell I'd give it to her. "No. I wasn't planning on since I was leaving."

"Now that you're not, you must have one."

I wiped my face with my hands. "Fine. I'll choose one of the brothers on the next Church."

"I want it."

Here it is.

Taking a long breath, I ran all my fingers through my hair and set my hands behind my head. I loved Cameron to death, but she was testing me and my patience in fucking dangerous ways.

Ridiculously, though, for whatever fucked up reason, her bossy, stern tone and that cold face were making me horny as fuck. Suddenly feeling too hot, I took off my cut and t-shirt.

She stared at me with the same coldness. I was boiling, and she looked like a fucking robot. "Why are you taking off your clothes?"

I undid my belt and threw it on the floor.

"Dusty?"

Holding her gaze, I unzipped my jeans and boots and kicked them off me. Then I stood in my boxers in front of her, relieved my cock had some room to breathe.

She did look at my erection that peeked at her—for a very brief moment before she tore her eyes away, but she did look. "If you expect me to—"

"I didn't expect anything." I carried the duffle bag and kneeled in front of her. "I hoped. 'Cause I fucking miss you."

It was a moment before she looked at me again.

"I know I'm a douche sometimes…well, most of the time, but I get it. How…you were hurt. You'll need time." My voice cracked at the end as rage bubbled inside me.

She tucked her hair behind her ear. The slight shake in her fingers and the tightness of her jaws squeezed my heart. "Good."

"Wanna see the stuff I got you?"

"You got me stuff?"

I unzipped the bag and got out the new outfits I bought. "Although you look super fucking hot in my clothes, and I'm never gonna wash them, you can't keep wearing them."

She took in the tops and jeans, her eyes brightening a little bit. "You went shopping for me?"

"Yup. I got you some boots, bras and underwear as well. You can't wander around the brothers commando like this." I dug in the bag and got a little, white box. "I also got you a phone. The old one is broken. You can't use it after the attack anyway."

A tiny smile crossed her lips. "That's very thoughtful of you. Thank you."

Her hand touched mine as she took the box. I twined my fingers with hers and brought her hand to my lips.

She quickly pulled her hand from mine. "What else is in the bag?"

I filled my chest with air, ignoring her reaction to my touch, reminding myself to be patient. Then I smirked playfully. "Does the duffle bag bring any memories?"

Her gaze dropped to the bag, her brows tied. "Really?"

"Yes." My skin tingled. "You're angry, Cammie. You need to let it out."

Something flicked in her big brown eyes. "You want me to let it out like this? On you?"

"Hell yeah." I'd gladly beg for it, too.

"I don't feel mad, Dusty. I should be, but I don't feel it. But if I did, I wouldn't be mad at *you*."

"Maybe, but I still want you to take it all out on me. So use me, baby. I'm here for you. There's nothing in the world that I wouldn't do for you." I took her hand in mine again. "Please."

She didn't take it away this time. She peeked at the BDSM toys in the bag. "If I use these on you…now…when I'm like this…I'll hurt you." Her eyes returned on me. "Really bad."

I swallowed, my dick swelling at the thought alone. The threat. The danger. The anticipated rush. "I deserve it."

The same look she had when I ordered Chain and Serial to go stand on the roof glazed over her eyes. She wanted this as much as I did. Her perfect nipples confirmed it.

She didn't speak right away, and she seemed to be struggling with something. Her afflicted conscience, I assumed. "No, you don't. I don't blame you for what happened. It wasn't your fault."

Yes, it was. I didn't get out in time. I let the darkness get the best of me and drove her away. I left when I should have stayed. I didn't protect her from the monsters I trusted and called my family.

Everything was my fault, and I deserved to be punished.

"I blame myself." My eyes pleaded with her. "I really need this, Cammie." I squeezed her hand. "I need you."

CHAPTER 28

DUSTY

Cameron took one last look at the duffle bag before the last wall of her resistance fell down. "Strip."

My cock and heart leapt at her command. "Yes, Mistress."

She chose a collar and wrist cuffs and tossed them at me. "Put the collar on and cuff yourself to the bed." She picked some rope and a whip, and then she eyed me as I stood naked in front of her, my hard-on untamed.

Her eyes and voice were devoid of emotion. It hurt me to see this beautiful girl who opened her heart to a guy like me, the girl who, without thinking, hugged her captive when he started shaking, shut down like this. She'd been through a lot, enough darkness to swallow big men whole. How much could a person take anyway? It was only a matter of time before Cameron closed down and became the woman I saw now.

"What are you waiting for? I want you on all fours on the bed, collared, cuffed, ass in the air. Now."

On all fours? She wouldn't even look at me?

I didn't like it, but I obeyed. I was begging her to punish me, and she finally agreed. I couldn't back down when all I was trying to do was make her open up and feel again. She could hurt me all she wanted. If that was the price to feel back her love, I was ready to pay.

With the collar on as tight as possible around my neck, I went on my knees in the middle of the bed and cuffed one hand to the bed post while she did the other.

A shiver ran down my spine as I saw her hard eyes. They were hungry but not for love. For darkness a guy like me would feed. "Gonna tie my ankles, too?"

"Yes."

I grunted, a big twitch in my cock. "Thank you, Mistress."

The rope wrapped around my ankles, and then they were sprawled and tied immobile. She told me to move. I found it too hard to even shift on my knees.

She hovered around the bed, testing my restraints until she was satisfied. Her hair slid across my face as she bent to stare me in the eye, the whip in her fist. "We never played with a safeword. I think it's time to choose one."

My heart thrashed, but I shook my head. "I trust you."

"It has nothing to do with trust." She glided the back of the whip on my face. "Only pain."

If anyone knew anything about inflicting pain and what it did to people, how it brought the strongest of men to their knees, it would be me. And I wasn't by any chance a sadist. Now I was under the mercy of one, already on my knees, about to take all kinds of pain. By her.

For her.

Without thinking, the word fell of my tongue. "Annie."

Her head jerked back. A flicker of emotion twitched in her eyes when she heard her sister's name, but she smothered it the next instant with a clench to her jaws. "Annie it is."

Was it the right move to remind her of the one person she loved the most? The sister the Night Skulls kidnapped, raped and killed? Or a fucking mistake I was about to pay for?

The answer came heavy on my back. Three lashes that made me rattle the cuff chains.

"Are you sure this is what you want?" she asked, standing behind me.

The burn on my back hardened my cock. "Yes. Please."

"What if someone walks in or hears us? I know you have a different persona here. You're the one who tortures people not the other way around."

I hadn't thought about that. Come to think of it, it didn't really matter. I was still a Night Skull for one reason only. I didn't give a fuck about the way my brothers thought of me. "Not that I care, but I already locked the door. Owl is the only one allowed here anyway, and I wouldn't risk even him seeing you while we…"

"Fucked?"

That was what I was about to say. I didn't want her to think I was pushing her, though.

The whip swatted my feet. "I asked you a question."

I bit my lip on a groan. "Yes. I don't want anyone to see you while we fuck."

"Everyone does it in public here. Have you ever done that?"

I stared at the headboard. "Yes."

"You like it?"

"That was a long time ago."

Another swat seared my soles. Then the bed creaked, and I felt her weight on top of me from behind. She dropped the whip next to me and dug her fingers in my hair, yanking my head hard. "You like it?"

I swallowed, glancing up at her, as sweat trickled down my forehead and pre-cum leaked out of my cock. "I used to like to be watched, yes. But I'd never let anyone watch me with you."

"You'd kill anyone who watched me naked, wouldn't you?"

Her fucking rasp and the stare in her eyes were killing me. I'd nut on the bed like a school boy any time now. "Damn right I would. I'd kill any fucker who did as much as picture you naked or fantasize about your pussy."

She lowered her head to mine. Our foreheads touched, her hair all over me. My breath accelerated when she swiped her thumb across my mouth. Then her lips came so close to mine, melting me with their heat.

I reached for a kiss, but as soon as my lips touched hers, she held my lower lip between her teeth and bit me. I moaned, my every muscle tensing up. Then I moaned louder and louder until she stopped biting me.

"What if *I* like to be watched?" she whispered, her eyes fixed on mine.

Mine widened at the image she put in my head. "Is that really what you want?"

"I don't know. Never tried. Maybe I should."

My jaws clenched so hard my teeth would shatter.

She laughed. Giggled. Even though it was fake, it warmed my heart. Fuck, I was a lost cause when it came to any fucking gesture she made.

Her fingers left my hair, and my head fell back down. "The only thing I'd enjoy your *brothers* watch me do is…" She sighed. "Never mind."

The collar buckle chimed, and then the leather squeezed my neck. Heat pulsed through my face and cock. I rattled, pressure banging my head and ears. "Ca-mmie."

She didn't loosen her grip. My eyes rolled back as the veins in my neck throbbed. Lost in vertigo, I struggled to breathe. "Ca-mmie, pl-ea-se."

She wouldn't stop until all my body was shaking, and I was seriously on the edge of passing out. When she unbuckled the collar, I gasped for breath as if I had been drowning and just hit the surface.

Without enough time to recover, she choked me again until I felt my eyes were about to bleed. My fists clenched in the restraints. My whole body was on fire.

I didn't think I ever wanted her to ride my cock more than now.

When she finally stopped, my neck was collar-free, and the buckle thudded on the floor. "Thank you, Mistress," I managed, wishing I could say it to her face, not to a headboard.

"I choked you so hard it's going to leave marks. You sure that's okay?"

"Anything you do to me is okay." I'd tipped in sub space. Obviously.

She moved off me. Sudden cold replaced her beautiful warmth on my naked body. Then a chill ran down my ass as her fingertips drew circles on it. "Anything?"

When I didn't answer right away, she clawed her nails into my ass cheeks and squeezed the flesh in her grip.

"Fuck. Yes, Mistress. Anything."

Her palms soothed my burning cheeks before she ran a finger ever so softly between them. My ass clenched in reflex. Not sure what her next move would be. But I fucking loved how she was leaving me in shambles like that, pain and pleasure playing side by side in her game.

"Even if I claimed this virgin ass, right here, right now?" she whispered near my asshole, and I trembled.

My head was spinning. My cock was aching, desperate for her pussy, for her touch, for her anything. "If that's what you want, I'll take it."

She backed away in a snap. Shocked? I knew I was. A dildo up my ass was never a fantasy of mine. Not even a finger. Her finger. It just wasn't my kink. But right in this moment, I'd submit to her every will without hesitation.

That woman captivated me from the moment I'd laid eyes on her. She might have unchained me and got me out of her bunker, but she'd never really set me free. She would always be my captor, and I would always want to be her prisoner.

I never want her to let me go.

Something stirred behind me. Was she really going through with it? Fucking me in the ass? Claiming it? I tilted my head to the side, and I saw her sit on the bed. The next thing I knew she slid under me and her legs were stretched on either side of my knees. Relieved, I looked down, taking in her fucking body. Then my heart skipped a beat when I saw she'd lost the sweatpants, and her sweet pussy was naked inches away from my cock.

I yanked at the chains. "Fuck." I dragged my gaze back to her face. "Uncuff me. Please."

She held my stare, cupping my balls. "Why?"

I licked my lips, groaning. "I can fucking smell your pussy from here. I wanna eat it. I want my cock buried in it all night. Please. I can't take it anymore. Uncuff me."

"Make me your VP."

"What?" It was too hard to focus with the shit she was doing to my balls and the base of my shaft. And the juice glistening from her pussy.

"You said anything I did to you was okay."

I nodded. "But being my VP has nothing to do with—"

She started stroking my cock, and I pulsed in her fist. "You'd let me fuck your ass, but you won't let me be your VP?"

I blinked, evening my breaths. "I…I'm…" *Lost for words. Can't put two words together. About to fucking come.*

"You don't care about the MC anymore. You have nothing to lose here, so I'll make you a deal." She stopped stroking when I was just right over the edge. This denial hurt more than the lashes and the bites and the chokes. I seriously needed to come. My balls were about to explode.

"I become your VP," she rolled her palm over my balls, "if I'm good at it we stay." Then she squeezed hard enough to make me gasp. "But if I fuck up…we leave like you want."

I stared back at her, my jaw hanging in pain. She smiled, the smell of her pussy getting stronger. She fucking loved it. My pain. My helplessness. My submission. If I glanced down, I'd see juice dripping between her legs.

"What do you say, *Prez*?" she drawled the Prez part and freed my balls.

As if my soul had been shoved back into my chest, I moaned my answer. "Yes."

A victorious grin danced on her lips. Then she crushed them into mine. She had played me good. Got me where she wanted to get what she wanted with zero resistance.

I hated what she'd just done, using my need for her like this. But I fucking loved her for it. Her dark side spoke to me. Frightened me. As much as the good side always did.

She had always found a balance, though. Now, I wasn't so sure. I knew the look in her eyes by heart. I had seen it so many times before. With the brothers. With Roar and Rush. With Beth.

Cammie had tasted blood, and now she was thirsty for more.

If she screwed up, that deal I'd just made her, thinking with my fucking cock, could be our ticket out of this hell. If she didn't…

My ol'lady was the smartest person I'd ever known. She wouldn't screw up.

What the fuck had I done?

CHAPTER 29

CAMERON

I grabbed the keys and started to uncuff
Dusty. He left a trail of kisses on my bare ass
as I did. When his hands were free, the first
thing he did was pull me into his embrace.
Swiftly, I shrugged out of his arms and got off
the bed.

He rested his butt on his heels. "Come
back here."

I picked up my—his—sweatpants off the
floor and made a fool of myself trying to get
back into them with one hand.

"You can't seriously leave me like that?"
He gestured at his throbbing erection.

My eyes met his needy ones. I was about to explain why I would leave him without a release. How every time I looked into his eyes, the image of his fucking father on top of me, about to rape me, flashed in my head. How touching the only man my heart beat for now made my skin crawl. But I chose to lie instead. "It's the rest of your punishment. I think you're going to enjoy it."

"No." He shook his head vigorously. "I really don't. Baby, please come back here."

"Your cock was throbbing and swelling in my hand when I stopped right before you came. I really think you enjoy cum denial, Dusty."

He swore, but he seemed to have bought my lie. "What about you?"

"What about me?"

"You telling me you're not slick and wet right now?"

I was. Apparently, lust had nothing to do with turned-off emotions. I could feel nothing and still get soaking wet for playing with a hot man with a big fat cock. "I'll take care of myself."

"Let me take care of you," he begged. "I'll eat you real good. You know I would."

Tempted, I hesitated to refuse him. I wasn't bleeding anymore. The pain in my vagina was tolerable. The throbbing heat wasn't. I stared from him to the sweatpants. I couldn't put them on without help anyway.

"Please, Cammie. If you won't let me fuck you, at least, let me taste you. I fucking miss your taste."

I set the sweatpants on the bed and went to the duffle bag.

"More toys?" he asked.

I found a blindfold and gave it to him. "Put it on."

He felt the fabric in his hands. "But I wanna see the pink of your—"

"It's the only way I'm gonna let you near me." My voice went louder than I intended. Rougher.

He pursed his lips and silently put the blindfold across his eyes.

I knew I hurt him, not in a good way. I could see it in his eyes even when they were hidden. The brick wall that had been going higher around my heart since I woke up shielded me from the monstrous guilt. Of what I was doing to Dusty. Of what I did to Rush. Of what happened to Ashley.

I couldn't feel any of it now. I couldn't fall apart now. That wall was the only thing holding me up. That dark nothing felt good and right and perfect for what I'd planned to do with the rest of my life.

Posing under him, I took a deep breath and ushered his head between my legs. He nipped at my inner thigh before I even spread my legs. I reached to grip the headboard with both my hands, immediately reminded of the damn cast. I shifted my attention down on where his mouth was mere inches from my heated flesh.

"Oh," I sighed when his tongue swept over my clit.

Smiling against me as if I didn't hurt him a minute ago, he twisted his lips until he could suck more of me into his mouth. "So fucking sweet," he praised as his tongue slipped lower, lapping up my core.

I pulled his head closer, tightening my thighs around it. He knew I was about to choke him with this move, so he took a deep breath and dove in.

The licking, sucking, and tongue fucking went on relentlessly. He worked hard without stopping, devouring me for what seemed to be days.

"Oh fuck," I panted.

He pushed his head up, but then he plunged back down, as if he remembered he was blindfolded and couldn't see me. The wash of his warm breath over my sensitive clit drove me wild. I dug my fingers in his hair, yanking at the back.

He groaned and placed his palms under my ass, sucking, lapping, and swiping that talented tongue over my center, knowing exactly what it took to get me off. My pussy quivered against his mouth as loud, successive moans seeped out of my chest.

"Fuck. Yeah, baby. That's it." He licked me dry as I climaxed, squeezing my ass.

My thighs shook as I eased them off his head. This gorgeous man knew how to eat a girl, leave her boneless yet hungry for more.

CHAPTER 30

DUSTY

I took off the blindfold, licking the rest of her taste that lingered on my lips. The second Cameron looked into my eyes, she tensed and climbed off the bed. She didn't give me one considerate glance over her shoulder as she picked some new clothes and underwear. She didn't untie my ankles. She didn't offer to let me shower with her. Nothing.

She disappeared into the bathroom. Then, to add to all that shit, she locked the fucking door. The echo of the lock thudded in my chest and took what seemed to be forever to die down. I fumed, running murderous scenarios over and over in my head as I freed my legs, my fucking erection not cooling down.

I jerked off real quick so I could focus on other things than her pussy, strategize how things were going to play out when she came back into the room.

My sweet Cammie wasn't the kind of girl to use sex to get what she wanted and then leave like that. She wasn't the kind to treat me like a fucking fuck toy either. Even in our play. She got rough but never uncaring.

The new Cameron however...

She had this 'I care about shit and feel no shit' act that I couldn't bring myself to believe. Was that really who she'd become?

No. My sweet Cammie was still in there somehow. I could feel it.

Something was up with my girl, though. Not just the way she was dealing with what happened to her. Her diabolical mind was planning something, and I needed to get to the bottom of it.

It didn't mean I wasn't angry as fuck. I grabbed the t-shirt she was wearing to clean myself, but her smell that lingered in it tampered with my head. In a split-second, I turned from a raging bull to a romantic motherfucker hugging the fabric with closed eyes, filling my nostrils with her fucking smell.

The bathroom door unlocked, and I flinched, throwing the t-shirt away with a curse on my tongue.

She came out, fully dressed in blue jeans and top.

"That was quick," I said, and then I noticed her hair wasn't wet.

She took one glance at my glistening cock and the load I shot on the floor before she went to the dresser as if she had seen nothing. "I just washed up and changed. It's easier to get dressed by myself sitting on the toilet seat or the bathtub edge."

She had a point. I had broken one of the only two chairs in the room the other day. The only one left was made of leather. It stuck to the ass. I went after her. "Why won't you let me help you?"

Her gaze met mine in the mirror as she brushed her hair. "Because I hate to be treated like a baby. When do I get my patch?"

"What the…" The fumes returned to blaze me. "Not now."

She dropped the brush on the dresser and spun. "Why the fuck not?"

"'Cause no one can just waltz in and become VP. You're my ol'lady but not a

Night Skull. There are rules and initiation and—"

"I think we got that covered. Just put it to a vote or whatever."

"Even if I can do that, it's not the right fucking time. The brothers aren't going to like it."

"I don't care about them liking me."

"I don't want anything to disturb the Beth situation. If they turn their back on me now and gang up with her instead—"

"Then they weren't loyal in the first place and deserve the bullet."

I hated it when she was fucking right. "My men are loyal to me and the Night Skulls."

"Great. You have nothing to be afraid of then."

I wanted to thrust my cock into that mouth until she stopped talking all so smart. "I'm not afraid of anything!"

"As you shouldn't be. It's the *brothers* who should be afraid. The two men up the roof are the perfect example for what happens to those who even think of crossing you or me."

She had an answer for everything. I started to suspect the whole act of 'I wouldn't fuck you because I was hurt' was a ploy to entice. A strategically placed tactic to make me beg for her punishment and domination, when my resistance was non-existent, and she could get me to give her the fucking VP patch.

Could this really be true? *Is that all you care about, Cammie?*

I didn't know anything anymore. I couldn't think straight. Fury along with my stupid, endless, unhidden need for her clouded my mind. I fought so hard not to lay her on this very floor and push inside her until the only things that flared out of her mouth were moans and my fucking name.

She went back to brushing her hair. I was still naked, and she could see I was aching for her, but she grabbed the fucking brush instead of my cock. "You gotta announce it tonight because I need to know everything about the club as soon as possible. The *brothers* need to fill me in about the business, rival gangs, any threats, everything. Also what do we have on Beth so far?"

My hand reached for the brush, yanking it out of her grip. She stifled a yelp as I held her wrist. Then I pushed her until her back was on the wall and my breaths on her forehead.

Her tits rose and fell rapidly. Fire flickered in her eyes as I met her heated stare with one more smoldering, searching for answers to a million questions ripping me apart.

She just stared back at me as if she were made of stone and fire.

In this moment, all my questions were reduced to one. "Do you even love me anymore?"

"You're hurting my arm," she whispered on a thick swallow, but she didn't pull her eyes from mine.

Another fucking act.

My grip tightened around her wrist as my heart hammered in my chest. "I'm not. I know your body and how fucking strong you are more than anyone, so stop shitting me and answer my fucking question."

"I said you're hurting my arm!" Her knee shot up and smashed into my balls.

"FUCK!" I doubled over, holding my junk, cursing through the pain. The second I was able to straighten my back, I stepped away from her, my fist punching two holes in the wall. Two seconds later, I was in my jeans, my t-shirt, cut and boots in one hand, the other slamming the door shut behind me.

CHAPTER 31

CAMERON

I zipped up my new leather jacket the second I stepped out to the front porch. It was almost seven a.m., and the sun was nowhere to be seen on this foggy day. Last night, I was freezing to the bones and couldn't sleep. I convinced myself my insomnia had nothing to do with Dusty not being there. The cold was the only thing to blame.

Stepping off the porch, I noticed the sloppy scaffolding work. The amateurish thing could work on a hot day—it was only three-story high—but it wouldn't stand this weather. And from the look of it, the grey sky was ominous enough to confirm the storm that destroyed the roof wasn't over.

My arms crossed over my chest, my hands seeking warmth under my armpits, as I took a few steps and peered up at the roof. Fuck. Chain and Serial were still up there.

Petrified. Their faces pale in the fog. They must have been cold and starving, standing like this for more than twelve hours. Afraid, too. I could tell because they wouldn't even look back at me, their throats working on rough swallows.

For a split-second, I thought about telling them to come down, even if they wouldn't obey unless the order came from Dusty himself.

Did I just feel sorry for them?

The screen door swung open, the squeak snatching me—saving me—from the flicker of emotion sneaking up on me.

Owl appeared from the mist, looking more of a *raven* in all the leather. "What are you doing, princess?"

"Assessing the damage…not that's any of your business. What are *you* doing here this early? Are you watching me?"

"I don't sleep at night. They don't call me Owl for no reason." He towered over me.

"And yes, I'm watching you. More like watching over you."

"My guarding Owl," I scoffed, saving my breaths. Arguing that I didn't need a bodyguard would fall on deaf ears. Owl was just following orders.

I walked to the side of the house, inspecting the rest of the scaffolds. I pointed at a very fragile, unstable pole. "Someone's neck could wind up broken because of this one. All of these need to be redone."

He rolled his eyes at me. "The men will be done with the roof today at best. Nothing is gonna happen, princess."

Great. Even the doctor here is a fucktard.

I didn't know why I gave a shit anyway. It was the aspiring engineer in me who did, I presumed. As for me, I hoped all of them broke their necks, choked on their beers, rolled over their bikes or got fucking bullets in their ugly skulls.

"C'mon, buddy. Let's go," someone said from inside the house.

The screen door squeaked again, and a big man with red hair and a Road Captain patch on his back emerged. Then a little boy dragging a school bag flashed onto the porch.

I scowled as I watched him race to the parked bikes.

"Easy, buddy." The redhead laughed and nodded at Owl but not me. "He can't wait to get on the road."

Owl laughed back. "Stay in school, Kid!"

Yes. Stay in school. Stay the fuck out of here. Run and never look back. What the fuck was a child doing here?

"A snake bit you?" Owl asked.

I dragged my gaze from the cutest little boy who was now wearing a tiny helmet and getting on the redhead's bike. "What do you mean?"

"You look like you were bitten by a snake, princess."

I only realized my brows were hooked so tight from the headache pulsing in my forehead. "Who's that?"

"Skid and his son."

"He lives here?"

"Skid, yes. The boy is just crashing. Prez has a strict no kid lives here rule."

Finally something Dusty and I agreed on.

The gate opened and Skid's bike roared away. A wave of nausea hit me hard.

"Why is the boy's presence making you so grumpy?" Owl asked.

I was asking myself the same question. The lump in my throat and the squeeze around my heart were inexplicable.

Liar. You know exactly why you feel like shit right now.

The voice in my head had returned. The nagging asshole that kept calling me on my shit. Great. I gritted my teeth. "Can you make sure he doesn't play around here?"

His eyes narrowed at me, as if he'd finally seen my concern about the safety hazard. "Yeah."

I stomped away before he'd ask more questions or see through my shield. The boy hurting himself around the repairs was *one* of the reasons I felt like this—the least that mattered.

"Where are you going, princess?" His footsteps crunched the gravel behind me.

"Looking for Dusty."

"He's not here."

I spun on my heels. "I don't suppose you're gonna tell me where he is?"

He shook his head.

"Fuck you."

"That will get us both killed, princess."

My hand balled into a fist. "Whatever, asshole. And fucking stop calling me that. I wasn't born here."

He smirked. "Prez said to treat you like royalty. He also said you were allowed a ride if I came with you."

"*Allowed* me a ride?" I snorted a bitter laugh.

"Hey, you like you need one. I know I do. So why don't you just tag along and clear your head?"

Despite how enraged I was, I loved the idea of a ride. However, the last time I saw my Harley it was covered in piss and trash. "Well, I don't have a bike."

"Yours has been in the garage for days. But you can't ride with the cast."

"Wait, what?"

"Dusty sent two prospects to bring it here for a fix on the same day of the assault. It's running, clean and as shiny as new."

Thoughts spiraled in my head. I never asked Dusty what he was doing at my apartment that night when he was supposed to be here in Rosewood. The picture was getting clearer now. He did come to SLO to apologize like he said. He must have waited for me at school, and when I didn't show up, he called…Ash…and found out about the vandalizing. Then he sent for the prospects, waited for them to take the bike…

You're not Dusty. Ash's last words burned through my brain.

She knew he was coming. He must have told her. That was why she pretended to forget her purse so she wouldn't lock the door, easing the way for him to get in the apartment. That was why she waited a little until he'd have arrived before she returned. Perhaps she even got me that pregnancy test so I'd take it when Dusty was with me, so we could find out together and be happy. Only Dusty was late, and Rush was the one there, because Dusty was waiting for the fucking prospects…so he could do something nice…for me.

My chin quivered, and tears threatened to spill from my eyes. Swiftly, I snapped them shut, my nails spearing my own palms.

Not now. You can't fall down now. Please.

I pleaded with my brick wall, fighting back the tears. I needed the numbness. I needed the dark.

You need, Dusty.

I snarled like a wounded animal, my head lifted to the sky. The motherfucking voice was right as always. I did need Dusty. I needed to tell him it was not his fault. It was mine all along.

I'm the only one to be blamed for everything that happened.

And what shall happen.

CHAPTER 32

CAMERON

I settled for a ride on the back of Owl's dirt bike. The cast truly hindered my steering. I was surprised Dusty gave Owl permission to let me share the same ride. Ol'ladies weren't allowed on any bike but their ol'men's. Owl said *our* chapter was more lenient than others when it came to the club queen, courtesy of Roar and Beth. He'd always bent the rules for her, and it was ordinary for Dusty to do the same.

I'd also learned that Beth technically ran the club with Roar even when she didn't exactly patch in. She was the Treasurer of the club even without the colors.

The bitch might have granted me a favor without knowing.

After a short coastal drive, Owl moved smoothly around the bends of the motorcycle trail near Shoreline Park. The crispy air filled my lungs as I soaked up the calm scenery of the bay and the woods. It felt good to just be out there.

The drive up to the trail had taken over a couple of hours. I knew I'd be sore once I got off the bike, especially since a lot of the trail was bumpy and unpaved. Owl pulled the bike over in a little turnout that was marked with a picnic area sign. He turned off the bike and said, "I thought you could use a break."

I slipped off the bike and used his shoulder to steady myself. "Yeah, I think my legs need a stretch."

He nodded and stood up as I took off my helmet. "Mine too. You want to take a walk?"

Beyond the picnic tables there was a hiking trail that led up into the woods. The tree groves looked beautiful from here. "Yeah. I'd love that."

He secured the bike and started ahead of me. Once we were on the trail, he walked by my side. It was wide. There were garbage cans along the way and wood chips had been laid over the loamy earth.

A few minutes later, the path got narrower, winding, and full of twisted tree branches. They seemed untouched by man, and that appealed to me. I did love the smells of the earth. The way the new ones of the blooming foliage mixed with the old.

We followed the trail quietly. One thing I liked about Owl was that he wasn't full of shit and only spoke with measured words. He seemed to know I needed the quiet. He might have needed it, too.

As we gained elevation each step became spongier with the mud and dirt hugging our boots. The air got cooler, thanks to the thickness of the trees and foliage, the sun yet to be seen. Even the grey sky was disappearing above the umbrella of leaves and branches overhead. The only sounds were the occasional rustle of leaves as small woodland animals scurried through and the chirping of birds in the trees overhead.

Lost in the scenery, I didn't notice when Owl had veered off the trail and led me deeper into the thicket of trees. Any girl in my position should be afraid about being up here all alone with him. He could do anything to me, and without any sort of a weapon on me,

I'd be powerless to stop him. But I didn't have an ounce of fear in my body.

Good. The numbness was back. At least, if I died here, it would be peaceful, and I wouldn't feel anything.

"That's enough. We should get back," I said. My feelings were numb, but my mind was alert.

"There's a hidden meadow off the trail only a few of us know about. You should see it. It's not far from here."

"Dusty knows about it?"

He shook his head. "Don't think he does."

Shit.

Fuck me both ways and piss on my grave if that man with those kind blue eyes and fatherly figure aura turned out to be another dick Beth sucked and made into one of her pawns.

Had I turned too dumb overnight not to see that one coming? After all that had happened to me? Even my gut instinct that alarmed me about Rush when he tried to kidnap in the middle of the day didn't work?

Hell, it still wasn't working now, as if nothing in me accepted to believe Owl was *that kind* of a bad guy.

I slowed down, calculating whether my next step should be back or forth. When he realized I trailed behind him, he stopped and spun toward me. "You're okay there?"

"If you killed me here, it would probably take months for anyone to find my body."

He froze, his brows furrowed.

"I know you have your gun on you. I could feel it when I was on the bike behind you."

A chuckle came out of his mouth as he lowered his head. "Shit. I didn't think this through."

"What didn't you think through? How I'd figure you out or how you're gonna bury me? Because that would be a little problem…unless you already hid a shovel up there in the night…"

His laugh got louder. "Princess, you watch a lot of movies."

"Do I? So you're not really working for Beth and you didn't lure me down here to finish what she started?"

He shook his head, still laughing. "You probably think all of us are backstabbing motherfuckers, and I don't blame you. Bringing you here like this…" The blue eyes softened at me. "Sorry, princess. That meadow is my thinking spot. I only thought it was nice, and you could use a peaceful place. Didn't mean to spook you like that. Let's head back."

I stepped forward after all. "No."

"No? Why not?"

I shrugged. "I'm a sucker for meadows."

He cackled this time. Then he led me through the dark, cool forest—knowing where he was going—until the trees opened into a lush, green clearing, the most beautiful wildflower meadow at the end of it. Instantly, a peaceful feeling washed over me.

We sat under a grove on the meadow border, filling our lungs with the pure air for what seemed to be an eternity. Time meant absolutely nothing here.

"I've been nothing but a dick to you, but I'll never hurt you, Cameron," he suddenly said. "Just know that."

I glanced at him, but he was focused on the horizon. "I remind you of someone, don't I?"

His hand reached to the back of his jeans, bringing out a wallet. He opened it with a heavy sigh and showed it to me. A photo of a teenage girl with a beautiful smile was tucked inside. She had long brown hair and big brown eyes and didn't look older than sixteen.

"Your daughter?" I whispered.

"Her name was Kasey. She would have been twenty-six today."

Fuck. "How did she…"

"Ten years ago, on her birthday, she wanted to take my bike for a ride alone. I told her no and to wait for me until I finished my shift at the hospital. I promised her I wouldn't be late, and she waited for me... But I was late as always. Even on her fucking birthday." He glanced down at the photo. "She decided to go on her own, to punish me, I guess. The last time I saw her, she was on a gurney entering my ER. She died in my arms that night." Sniveling, he snapped the wallet shut and returned it to his pocket.

"I'm sorry." I wished I'd been able to say more, show him more. He needed compassion or he wouldn't have shared his story with me. "I truly am."

"The look in your eyes when you saw Skid's boy," he finally met my gaze, "I know it well."

"What look?"

"The 'no kid should ever die again' look. Don't pretend you're not hurt over your unborn baby."

"I'm not," I replied too fast.

"Denial will only get you this far. Then it will hurt like a motherfucker, leaving a hole in your chest that will never be filled. I got hung up on painkillers to numb the pain. I have a feeling that you'll do worse."

I jumped to my feet. "It's getting late. I wanna head back to Rosewood."

"You're a smart girl. Don't be too smart for your own good." He rose and held my gaze. "You and Dusty must get out of the MC while you still can. No kid should ever die again, Cameron."

CHAPTER 33

CAMERON

The gates to Rosewood opened for us, the wind blowing as loud as the bike roar. Owl helped me off the bike and said, "Please think about what I told you."

I didn't wait for him as he went to park the bike. I wanted to find Dusty to...to ask for my patch again. Secretly, what I really wanted was to know where he had been all night and if he was all right.

Starting to the clubhouse, I glanced at the roof. Disappointed to see Chain and Serial up there. That most likely meant Dusty hadn't returned yet to end their misery. The other men worked their way through the bricks and tiles while the assholes both looked like they were about to pass out…or cry.

My glance lowered to the fucking scaffolds, my engineer's mind refusing to let go and…

No, no, no, no! FUCK! "Owl!" I darted through the wind. "Get a mattress!"

"What?!" his voice trailed behind me.

I couldn't even look at him over my shoulder as I ran. My eyes were fixed on the little boy about to bite the dust. "A mattress! Hurry!"

Snap.

Yelp.

"Daddyyyyyy!"

The boy's squeal thudded in my heart as the unstable pole broke under his foot. He was hanging in the air, almost three-story high, nothing stopping him from falling but his little grip on the other piece of wood that was about to break as well.

Panting, I finally reached the side of the house. The men on the roof stopped working and were about to make everything worse.

"Nobody moves!" I stared at them, holding a warning hand. "The whole thing is about to collapse."

The boy started to cry, calling for Skid.

"Where's his father?" I asked.

"Out," one of the guys answered.

The boy's cries grew louder.

I smiled at him to soothe him a little. "It's okay. It's okay! You're not going to fall. But even if that happens, I'm right here, not going anywhere, and I'm gonna catch you. Okay, champ?"

He pursed his lips, nodding, tears dropping down his face as he did.

"What's your name? Can you tell me your name?"

"Carter," he whimpered.

"Okay, Carter. I need you to hold really tight, but I need you to stop swinging your body. Can you do that for me?"

"I guess," he whimpered again. "My hand is really slippery. Can I use the other one please?"

Oh my God. He spoke as if he was asking for more candy. "I'm sorry, champ, but you're gonna have to hold tight with that slippery hand, just for a few more seconds. I know you can do it. You're so strong." My head whipped to the front door. "OWL!" Fuck. I returned my gaze to the boy. "How high can you count, Carter?"

"One hundred."

"Wow. That's so cool. Can you start counting for me?"

He did as I asked him. Only I knew he wouldn't make it to twenty before the wood in his grip broke. My eyes inspected the rest of the interconnected poles, looking for the strongest parts that could take more pressure. However, as the wind rattled the trees, and the crappy poles shook violently, my hopes to climb up and get Carter thinned.

"Eleven, twelve…"

Shit. Thunder rumbled in the sky and rain poured on us. Any second now the whole scaffolding was going to take the boy and fall on top of me. The only way I could save him was that fucking mattress. I glanced one last time at the front door. "Owl, I need that mattress now!"

"Fifteen, sixteen…"

FUCK!

Desperately, I glanced at Carter's wet hazel eyes, my heart rocketing hard. "Carter…just jump." I roughly calculated the distance to where he was about to land when he'd jump, positioned myself there and spread my arms in the rain. "I'm gonna catch you."

"Jump?" Carter asked, the men on the roof mumbling I was crazy.

I silenced the men with one pointed look. Then I focused only on Carter, the rain dripping over my hair and face. "Yes, baby. Don't be afraid. I'm right here."

Something I wished I'd had a chance to say to my sister, my friend, my own baby that would have been just as cute and adorable and innocent as this little boy.

Carter let go of the pole that snapped the next instant, and everything moved in slow motion and at light speed at the same time.

He landed safely in my arms, and I screamed at the shattering pain under the cast. The next thing I saw was ropes flying off the scaffolds and poles, inclining and collapsing, about to hit us in the head.

I held carter tightly and twisted, shielding him with my body as I jumped in the air to the side as far as possible from the falling poles. I shut my eyes, preparing myself for the coming pain. The seconds seemed to be never-ending as I waited to hit the ground.

Finally, I hit a surface. Then everything went black.

CHAPTER 34

CAMERON

"I'm fine. You go check on Carter," I told Owl as he laid me on a table in a dark room, an X-ray machine next to me.

I didn't know when Owl had arrived or placed the mattress on the ground down the porch. But I was thankful he did it just in time. Even though the scaffolds barely touched Carter as I rolled us over, without the mattress, my weight and the impact of the fall could have caused serious damages to Carter's tiny body.

Owl ignored what I'd said and kept positioning me for scanning. "He's perfectly fine. Not a scratch, thanks to you. It's your head and arm that I'm worried about."

My head pulsed with a hollow echo, and shooting pain seared my arm. I sighed, rolling on my side. "Did you see Dusty's bike when you were parking yours?"

"No, princess. He's not here yet." He repositioned the machine head. "Stay still."

"Can we not tell him about what happened?" I chanced.

He snorted.

It was worth the shot. "It's your ass I'm worried about."

"I deserve whatever he does to me." His voice went all bleak. "Now stop talking and stay still."

When I got out of the dark room, I realized I was on the upper floor of the clubhouse. Skid, another redhead and Carter gathered downstairs.

"Cameron!" the boy squealed and ran up the stairs, and then he flung his arms around my knees in the most adorable of hugs. I squatted to wrap my good arm around him. He buried his head in my shoulder.

My heart fluttered. I couldn't help kissing his little head and rubbing it playfully. When I looked up, his father was there.

I lifted myself up, my whole body sore. At full height, my head was at the level of Skid's upper arm, not even his shoulder. He had long, red hair, but his face was shaved. His eyes the color of honey. His nose crooked. His lips…distracting.

Damn men with cuts.

They were menacing and ugly yet attractive. Always had sexy fucking something that distracted from their truth.

He opened his mouth, and I noticed he had a couple of molars missing, and the rest of his teeth were crooked like the nose. But I was sure any other girl wouldn't even see any of that when she laid eyes on those lips.

"Thank you for saving my boy," he said.

"Of course."

"Church!"

My head jerked at Dusty's voice that boomed from downstairs. He was standing at the entrance with a big, bald man, his eyes fuming at me, a cigarette dangling from his mouth.

Skid kissed his boy and told him to stay with me. As Owl emerged from the X-ray room, Dusty came up the stairs with the scary Skull.

I looked at my boyfriend with anticipation, but he glared at me as he walked by me without a word. The three men followed him into a room down the hall.

CHAPTER 35

DUSTY

What the fuck was she doing up here? I fell into the chair at the head of my table, dragging a long breath from my cigarette. The brothers took their places, and I fought the urge to smash Skid's face for talking to my ol'lady without permission.

His jaws were tight, and he wasn't looking me in the face. The fucker was hiding something. After the meeting, I'd rip his tongue out of his throat to know what the fuck was going on.

"Someone is lacing our powder," I started. "There's been an OD. The stuff came from one of ours."

"No runner of ours would dare mess with the dope. The Lanzas' dope," Skid said.

Owl's eyes grew serious at me. "Unless they were promised something big in return."

"Exactly." I crossed my arms over my chest. "Big enough not to make them snitch even under Big Gun's knife."

Skip rubbed his face. "Beth doesn't have the power or the money to pull any of that shit. And why the fuck would she mess with our business and the fucking Mob?"

"She must have found a new home," I said.

"She fell on Wrench's lap already?" Owl's nose crinkled like he'd smelled a fart.

"There's no news from Detroit. No sign of Beth whatsoever there," Skid insisted. "Even the drivers we gutted the other day confirmed she didn't spend more than thirty minutes with Wrench."

"He is the one fucker who wants this chapter the most. He's been looking for a way to expand to the West coast for years. It makes sense if he's the one messing with our shit to take over," Owl explained. "And thirty minutes...with Beth's—"

I was about to grab his neck—it was still my fucking mother's pussy he was talking about—when Cameron barged in.

"What the fuck you think you're doing here?!" I snapped.

As if I said nothing, she closed the door and took a seat across the table.

"What the—" I bit my lower lip, my upper one curling in a snarl. "Cameron, would you for fuck's sake get the hell out of here, *please*?"

Snickers twitched the guys' mouths as they all looked down. They wouldn't look at her in front of me but behind my back... *These motherfuckers.*

"How polite of you to say please, *Prez*," she mocked.

I banged my fist on the table. "What the fuck do you want right now?"

"I came to collect my patch."

"What fucking patch?" I knew exactly what *fucking patch*.

All eyes were on me now, asking the same question.

"The VP patch. You said you'd announce it to the brothers at your next meeting? Have you announced it yet or were you saving it for the end?" she challenged.

Big Gun narrowed his eyes at me. "You're making your old lady your VP?"

Owl shook his head. "No way, Prez."

The only man who wasn't grumbling was Skid.

Wildfire blazed under my skin. I was angry for so many fucking reasons not one. First, Cameron was twisting my arm in front of my men. Second, my men were arguing with something I said I'd do. I didn't like the idea of giving her that patch, and after what she did last night, I decided to back out on our deal. But that was my place, not theirs. No one would've dared argue with Roar in fear of getting their heads blown off.

Third, the new fucking secret between my ol'lady and my fucking Road Captain.

"We have a deal," she reminded me.

"The deal is off," I seethed and smashed my cigarette under my boot.

"Is that how you do business around here?"

I pressed my palms on the table top and leaned forward, my stare piercing into hers. "Here, I do whatever the fuck I want."

She cocked a brow, standing from her chair. My dick twitched in my jeans as her whole body came into my sight. Fuck this shit. And fuck her for doing this shit to me.

"Let me ask you a question?" She looked around the room, slowly making eye contact with each man, not intimidated by anything or anyone. "How does someone become the president of an MC if they don't like the current one?"

Fucks and shits flared in the room. The men jumped to their feet, Big Gun, pulling out his piece. Reflexively, my arm spread in its range, aiming to lower it. I retracted it fast before anyone saw it.

The smirk on her face meant she did see it. She held her hands up. "At ease, soldiers, I'm unarmed."

Big Gun looked at me, and I nodded once fast, a glare on my face. *No one raises a gun at my ol'lady, even if she's pointing one at me.*

He lowered his hand and gave me an apologizing stare.

"I didn't know deals meant shit around here, so I was just asking if the same *off the president become the president* rule applies to VPs as well." She shrugged. "I've already done that part."

"Fuck," Owl mumbled.

Skid cleared his throat. "Well…a deal is a deal, Prez."

"Shut the fuck up! Everybody out! Now!" I exploded.

Chairs wheezed, and the door locked behind the three men in a flash. I crossed the room in two strides.

She gave me that look that brought me to my knees in the bedroom. *Not here, sweetheart.* In this room, I was the one who called the shots. "You played me for that deal. That's why it's off. If you dare barge in here like this again, I swear—"

"What? You're gonna hit me again?"

"Stop pushing my buttons," I ground the words under my teeth. "I didn't hit you. You know I'll never hurt you...or any woman."

"Pushing me to a wall, pulling your knife on your bitches when you want information, vowing to torture your mother and end her life isn't hurting women?"

I'm done being played by you. I stared at her mouth and those fucking lips, the need to tear them up with my devouring kisses and then punish them with my cock taking over me. "If you don't stop, I'll have a better use for that mouth of yours."

How dare you? jumped all over her face. Then her stare turned defiant. "Yeah?"

I leaned closer, my hand gripping the armrest of her chair instead of her ass as I really wanted. "Oh yeah. And there's a lot where that comes from. You gotta stop if you don't wanna be punished. I didn't push you like that, and you know it. How I get information is my business and my business alone. If you were born here, you'd know cock and violence are the only languages bitches understand. I chose to use the one that hurt me but didn't hurt *you*.

"As for Beth, she stopped being anything but the cunt that killed my baby before it had a chance to breathe. Not only does she have to pay the price, but she's also a traitor and a threat that must be eliminated." I unlocked the door. "Now get the fuck out. *Please.*"

She pushed it shut in the anxious yet snickering men's faces.

"If I get out of here without my VP patch, I'll leave Rosewood to find Beth and kill her myself," she threatened. "You don't seem to be doing a great job finding her on your own anyway."

For fuck's sake. I leaned back, my blood boiling. "Not if I lock you up."

"You really think that's gonna stop *me*?"

"Yes. I know how to fuck it out of you."

"Fucking try!"

I growled, both my hands on her waist, lifting her and setting her on the table. My lips mashed against hers as I unzipped her jacket. She purred in my mouth, pushing me off.

The pink flesh of her chest and the pebbling nipples called to me. I slid her forward and spread between her thighs as I pushed into her. She moaned as she felt my hard-on.

"Tell me you want me as much as I want you?" I demanded.

"I don't."

I ate her tits with my stare. "Nipples don't lie, Cammie. Or are you just cold?"

"You're an asshole."

I cupped her tits and squeezed hard. My cock, achingly hard, throbbed in need.

She pushed my hands away. "Stop touching me."

"Your heart is racing. Your breath is catching. Is it out of fear or love?"

Her jaws hardened as did her stare.

I unzipped my jeans and pushed inside her. She was so slick the whole tip went in. "Fear or love, Cammie?"

When she didn't answer, I pushed my shaft to the middle of my Jacob's Ladder inside her wet pussy, and asked again.

"Fuck you, Dusty."

"Fuck you, Cameron." I went all in, fisting her hair, and slammed into her, taking what was mine, what she thought she could deny me. "Answer me." I asked between thrusts.

"Fear or love?" My cock throbbed inside her, the feeling of her wetness I'd been missing for weeks so fucking good. "Answer me, goddammit."

"I'm not afraid of you," she moaned.

I smiled against my will and kissed her again.

"Stop. Touching. Me."

Fury returned to burn me. She wouldn't let me have a nice moment with her. "Don't ever tell me to stop touching you. You're mine. No matter what happens in this fucking world, no matter how much you love or hate me, you're mine. In here, you're my fucking property. I'll fuck you when I want wherever I want."

"Stop it!"

"Why?! If I just thrust one more time inside, you'll cover me with cum. So why the fuck don't you want me to touch you?"

"I want you, Dusty. I just…"

"You just can't look at my fucking face while I'm near you." I finished for her, a thousand blades slicing at my heart. "You want to look at my fucking Road Captain instead."

"What?!"

"Don't even think about lying. I see the way he looks at you." I kicked the table leg.

"I'll kill him right in front of you before he even thinks about touching you."

Her jaw hung low. "I met the guy thirty minutes ago. Right before you came in. Don't get crazy."

"It's you and your fucking blindfold that's driving me crazy," I said under my breath. "Why can't you look in my eyes when I…"

The words got stuck in my throat. My eyes narrowed with suspicion, and then with realization. I froze in place, a rock stuck in my throat. "Jesus, baby."

Her eyes glistened. "I didn't want to say anything because I didn't want to hurt you," she said. "I just need time."

I squeezed her shoulder as I pulled out, my head down, my engorged cock angry at me, a dull pain weighing down on me.

"Dusty—"

"I'll always have his eyes."

"Hey." She lifted my chin with her finger, making sure our gazes met. "I'll get over it." Her rasp thickened. "I promise."

"I should have killed that motherfucker myself."

Her head shook. "I did exactly what I was supposed to do. All I want is that patch so I can help get that bitch and end her like I ended him."

"You liked the feeling? Is that what it is? You're on a killing spree?"

She dropped her finger. "Liked? You think I killed Rush before you did it because it felt good?"

"I don't know what to think anymore. It hurts me to see you like this. It's like I'm looking at someone I've never known."

Her palm rested on my heart, sending a sweet chill down my back. "I did it for you, Dusty."

Wincing, I held her face in my hands. "Why?"

"When you killed Roar thinking he was your dad," she whispered, "you never got over it, no matter how hard you tried to convince yourself and me that you did the right thing to save me and had no regrets. The last night we were together before the assault, you blamed me for it."

"Cammie, I—"

She put her finger on lips, shushing me. "I'm not mad. I know you didn't mean it, but you can't help it. I will never forgive myself for what happened to Annie, and I'm not the one who put a bullet in her head. That kind of burden weighs on you so heavily sometimes it's too hard to fucking breathe. I didn't want it on you, Dusty. It was a relief to know that when you took Roar's life, it wasn't your dad's. I didn't want you to carry that burden again. Call Rush whatever you want, but he was your father. That's why *I* pulled that trigger, and why *I* will be the one pulling the trigger on Beth."

My shoulders slumped in defeat. I didn't know what to say to this.

"Give me my patch, Dusty. Let's get it all over with and move on."

CHAPTER 36

DUSTY

Shaking my head, I gave up. "Fine. You wanna run the fucking place, be my guest."

I opened the door. Then I gestured for the brothers to come back in. "Tell my ol'lady everything about the titty bar, the whores, the dope, the guns, the fucking Italians, Wrench and the other rivals," I spat, hoping to intimidate her.

Cameron didn't bat an eye.

"That's a lot to dump on your ol'lady in one sitting," Owl mumbled.

"I'm right here, and you don't see me complaining. I'm all ears," she said.

"But you're not a member of this club," he said. "You don't ride, and you have no miles. Not to mention, you have no colors whatsoever. I've been running for the Skulls for years and I only earned my patch and a right to this table a few months ago."

"Beth didn't have any colors either and yet she had the same rank you hold now, Owl? Hasn't this chapter always been *lenient* when it comes to Prez's ol'lady? At least, this ol'lady didn't betray the club or run away, not after she's been tortured, assaulted and raped by two former *members* and had to have blood on her hands to stop them because no other brothers did." Her eyes darkened, and she swallowed before she added, "Not even after she…lost her baby, the Prez's baby, because of it."

If she'd stabbed me with a blunt knife for every word she said, it'd have hurt less. I lit another cigarette and let the smoke prick my eyes. "After you fill her in on the business, we'll cast a vote."

My men stared at me in silence. What else would they say after she showed us all how much we failed to protect her and my baby?

"Nothing you're gonna tell me about the business is gonna change my mind or push me away," she said. "Since Roar took Annie,

I've had a pretty good idea about the nature of your activities, and I'm aware of all the properties the club owns. As for the Lanzas, I'm friends with their capo's wife. They owe me one, by the way. You know when I went to them for help, and they didn't tell me my sister was already dead then left me to spiral for months instead and almost lost my life because of it. Yeah, that can come in handy if you want to pull favors." She crossed her legs with a smirk. "I'm ready for your votes now."

I had no more cards to play to save her from the darkness that had dug its claws in her. I knew how stubborn she was, how much pain she was in, and how nothing but ruin would satisfy her. "Cameron Delaney, road name yet to be chosen, asks to patch in the Night Skulls, San Francisco chapter. What do you say?"

All except Owl said yes.

"In the matter of appointing a new VP," I blew out a long puff of smoke, "I name Cameron for the position. What do you say?"

"Yea," Skid said.

"Nay," Owl objected.

That left Big Gun's vote.

My Enforcer stared at me for guidance. My brothers and I understood each other without words. He must have known how fucked up I felt to be in this position. If he said yes, she'd be the VP. If he objected, it'd be a tie, and it'd be all on me to make that call. I made a deal with Cameron. I wouldn't be able to say no.

It didn't really matter who sentenced her to her coveted doom. Whether I was the one to announce it or someone else, it was me who dragged her down to hell right from the start.

"Nay," Big Gun finally said.

Cameron held my gaze in challenge. "We have a deal, Dusty."

It was tempting to say no. It didn't matter if I pissed her off about the deal. My only concern was that she was crazy and stubborn enough to break out and go find Beth herself. She'd be in danger without me protecting her. I'd never let that happen again. "There's no going back from here, Cammie. You sure this is what you want?"

Her stare didn't falter. "I'm all in."

I put out the cigarette, looking down at the table, my heart in shreds. "Owl, if you need help with the books, VP is your gal." I glanced up at her. "Congratulations."

She smiled, her eyes sparkling in triumph. "Thank you."

"When you're all done filling her in, someone better fucking tell me what happened to the scaffolds and why there's a mattress lying outside my porch."

CHAPTER 37

DUSTY

Cameron's arm was more fucked up after she'd rescued Carter. It didn't stop her from anything or even slowed her down. She thrived as the VP. In a matter of a week, she was running the brothers better than Rush himself. Skid was in debt to her for saving Carter. Owl already treated her like his daughter even when he was never on board with having her anywhere near the business. And Big Gun… They had become besties after going on her first raid.

"Your old lady is a badass." He had to tell me that when they returned that day. I didn't need to hear the details to know her sadist side clicked with his on the spot. Fuck, even Chain and Serial were kissing her boots when she let them off the roof.

It was the whores she had trouble with. They were jealous, and they hated her. She was too strict on them, and I was sure she hated them back.

I didn't give a shit about it, though. What really concerned me was how every day with every plan she made and every raid she went on, a piece of her died.

When all of this was over, would there be anything left of her heart or soul? Would there be enough to start a life away from all the blood? To be able to look at me again?

The questions spun in my head as any kind of a future together away from all the darkness seemed out of reach. She sat next to me in Church while explaining her new plan to find Beth.

"Beth isn't contacting her whores as we hoped. Every lead we got ended in pulling useless prospects' teeth and gutting junkies. Even the bounty on her head resulted in shit. This isn't working," she said.

"She is not in Detroit, if that's what you're saying" Skid said. "I spoke with Wrench myself, offered him a lot than he could refuse.

If he had her, he would have given her up by now."

"Same with all the other chapters," Owl added. Today was his first day out of the doghouse. I liked the motherfucker, but he had to be punished for not listening to Cammie and putting her life and the kid's in danger.

"I don't think she's in Detroit. From what you're telling me, Wrench isn't that stupid to keep her there. That doesn't mean he's not protecting her either," she said.

"What are saying, Claws?" Big Gun asked.

I fucking hated that road name. She wanted to go by Ninjaneer, but when everybody started laughing, she settled for Claws. Something Owl said to her once or some shit like that.

"Beth is either hiding at a rival gang or the son of a bitch is paying a lot more than our bounty to lace our dope, protect the bitch and buy everybody's silence," she answered.

"Prez?" Skid asked.

"It'd make sense if Detroit, like Chicago and the Midwest, wasn't ruled by more Italians. The Bellomos. Tino Bellomo is the Lanzas' strongest ally in the country. He won't sabotage Cosimo's operation. Our crack comes from the Lanzas, who get it directly from the cartel." I glanced at Cameron with a smirk. "As you may know, Carlos Alfarez, your *friend* and Cosimo's father-in-law, facilitates the whole thing."

She rolled her eyes, twisting her lips. "I haven't spoken to the guy since he got you out of my bunker, and as far as I know, he got out of the business and they let him because of Bianca, but if you want me to speak to him to see what he can find..."

"You can, but that's not my point. The point is Wrench doesn't have the money or power to go over Tino Bellomo or the Lanzas. He can't be the one lacing our crack. The rival MCs on the West Coast aren't stupid to mess with us either. Our chapter owns this part of the country, and the Night Skulls have more chapters than all of them together. Besides, we're the club operating for the Mafia. Even if they dare piss in our shit because of the recent shakes and betrayal, thinking they can swoop down on us, they won't dare mess with the Italians or the cartel."

"If Wrench is out of the game, that leaves Kentucky where she was last spotted," Skid says.

"I contacted the Wicked Warriors myself." That MC controlled Kentucky, and I'd made some friends from their chapter in Italy last year when I left after Annie. "Beth hasn't made contact with them. She's nowhere to be seen in Kentucky, and Jesse Savage has no intention or reason to fuck with us. I say she came back here, hiding under our fucking noses in plain sight."

"Or Wrench is helping her to make you think exactly that," Cameron said. "Wrench might have nothing to do with the powder, but he can be the one hiding Beth. You can't rule that out. He accepted a bribe before, even when he hated her and wanted her dead. Why wouldn't he do it again when you already offered him something he couldn't refuse?"

"Because he's promised something bigger," Owl answered.

"Exactly. Beth could be conspiring with him as we speak, promising him a permanent cut from our chapter if he, for example, gets rid of me," she said.

Or to take over the whole chapter after killing my ol'lady, and force me to fall in line or get kicked out. I won't be able to fight them alone without my brothers and crew, who she wouldn't mind having them murdered, too. There's nothing Beth wouldn't do to stay the queen of the Night Skulls. I looked at her. "I'm assuming you have a counterplan?"

She smirked. "More raids on the rivals on the West Coast…in Detroit patches."

Fuck.

The chin and beard scratching started around. Then all eyes darted at me.

"What do you want us to do, Prez?"

Creating feuds to cost Wrench any chance to set foot here and put pressure on him to release Beth was a great plan. Only if he was the one protecting her. But if he wasn't, he would retaliate. Bad.

I wiped a hand over my mouth. "Give us a minute."

"You don't like it?" she asked the second the brothers left.

"It's a diabolical plan that would backfire with an ugly mess if Wrench has nothing to do with Beth."

She shrugged. "What's the best he can do?"

"Raze Rosewood to the ground."

"So? You don't give a shit about Rosewood or the Night Skulls."

"I care about you and the rest of my brothers who are loyal to me. Skid has a kid for fuck's sake. Owl is my best friend and Big Gun would die for me. I don't want any of you to get hurt."

"We won't. Let that bastard come. We'll be ready for him and his Skulls." She patted my shoulder. "Think about it, Dusty. It's killing two birds with one stone. You might get what you want after all."

I took in her face that kept changing daily. The features were the same, but the psyche underneath... "I want to leave with you and never look back, but I don't want my men dead. I'm not Beth, and neither are you."

She sat on my lap and gave me a kiss, scrambling my thoughts. She'd barely touched me all week without the blindfold. "It's gonna work, *Prez.* I have a good feeling about it."

I loved to hear my title with her rasp. I nodded, tasting her lips again. "How about you talk to Alfarez, and I'll meet Cosimo before anything? Let's find out who's fucking our stuff first."

CHAPTER 38

DUSTY

When Cosimo showed up without his twin brother, I knew something was off. Enzio was his underboss, enforcer and sidekick. Cosimo never went anywhere without him.

I approached with Owl and Skid as Cosimo got out of his car, his bodyguards securing the woods.

"Tell me you have something," Cosimo said.

"We don't believe it's Detroit. It's something bigger. Big enough to fuck with you and the cartel, not just us," I said, expecting a threat or an outburst in response.

Cosimo was calm, not the kind of calm that intimidated people but pensive and somber. It was as if he knew what I was going to say before I said, as if he had a pretty good idea who was the fucker we were looking for.

"If Beth was the puppeteer, you have my word I—"

"You don't have to give me your word. I know you'll take care of her. It's better you than the Chopping Block."

I'd always heard horror stories about the Lanzas'—Enzio Lanza's—torture room. Cosimo's twin brother street name was Il Tagliatore. The Cutter. He did sick shit with his knife. His reputation never succeeded to shake me, though. I didn't think he had anything on Roar or Big Gun. With Cammie in charge of the Boiler, the Lanzas finding Beth first would be mercy for her.

"I need a favor, Cosimo," I said.

"I can't help you find her."

"Why not? It's your business like it's ours. I'm short on men, and your help can—"

He gestured for me to come closer. "Walk with me."

Skid and Owl shifted on their feet, fully alert.

CAMERON

"I need a word capo to capo. My men will stay with yours and we can all still see each other," Cosimo said.

I nodded at my brothers and walked with the man. It wasn't easy to trust anyone when your own parents betrayed you, but I knew Cosimo had something important to say that no one should hear but me, especially when it came to our deal about my leaving the MC.

"I have a lot to deal with in the family, Dusty. Yours might not the only one with a traitor," he started as soon as we were away from the men's hearing range.

"You think the crack lacing is an inside job? Why?"

"Why do you think?"

"Someone is after your seat."

He gave a terse nod. "You understand now I have a much bigger fish to fry and can't spare any men to look for your mamma. Betrayal hurts, and when it comes from family…" His fists clenched. "You know the feeling."

I wiped my hand over my mouth. "I'll find her, Cosimo. You have my word."

"Whoever catches their *buscetta* first updates the other?"

"Deal. I just need to know one thing. Rush was so sure I wasn't going to kill him when I found out his dirty. He had something. Did you talk?"

"I haven't seen him since that night you talked to me about making him your replacement. I haven't seen or spoken to your mamma either, but I'll look into it and let you know if it's related."

I nodded once. "See ya, Capo."

He shook my hand. "Will you still leave after it's over?"

If it were up to me, I would without a second thought. But it looked like I had a long way before I saved my girl from the darkness that wrapped around her like a cloak, feeding on her every second.

He patted my shoulder, bringing me into a hug. Then he whispered, "Do it. Don't let it suck you until there's nothing left. I still have your back." When he released me, the look in his eyes set my instincts on haywire. "A lot is going to change in the next few days. Be prepared."

CHAPTER 39

DUSTY

Two days later I found out why that look in Cosimo's eyes was ominous.

"He was the traitor after all. Can you believe this shit?" Skid snorted over beers. "Their capo himself was the one sabotaging their business? If you ask me, he got what he deserved."

"Who killed the switch on the bastard?" Owl asked.

Skid leaned closer, as if he was about to tell a secret, and snickered. "Enzio. His own fucking twin."

"No fucking way."

"The shit those fucking Italians have going on. Those two ate, pissed and fucked together, and look what the fuck happened."

"You turn your back on your brother, you get the bullet. Or in Cosimo's case, the Cutter's knife."

The banter along with the drinking kept going around me, but my mind was elsewhere. Enzio Lanza had murdered his twin brother, his capo, the leader of his family, in cold blood, and the reason? Cosimo Lanza was the one lacing the crack among several other sabotage missions of their family gun deals.

I couldn't wrap my mind around the fact that Cosimo was the one sabotaging his family from the inside. He was many things but a traitor? He ran the Lanzas for years, very successful ones, and he preached about family everywhere he went. Why the fuck would he destroy everything he worked so hard for?

Do it. Don't let it suck you until there's nothing left.

His encouragement behind my decision to leave the MC rang in my ear. From the last two meets I had with him, he was different, but in a way I never felt we were so similar. I could tell what was going through his head because I had the same thoughts. I fell in love and wanted to protect my woman more than anything even when it meant losing everything.

Cosimo must have felt the same way with his wife and son. He wanted to protect them from the life before the enemies and outside threats. Maybe, he, too, wanted out.

He wouldn't have betrayed his own blood for it, though. He would have found a replacement—he had a fucking twin underboss for fuck's sake—and left, just like I planned to. He wasn't stupid. Traitors never survived. He needed to live for his wife and son, who were now taken as fucking property by his brother.

Cosimo Lanza couldn't be the traitor.

"I beg to differ," Cameron said at Church.

"He said someone was after his seat. You should have seen the look in his eyes when I mentioned betrayal. He had someone in mind. He was planning on taking them down. They must have found out and said whatever fucking lies to the family and Enzio to off him before Cosimo killed them," I said. "Fuck, it could be Enzio himself."

She glanced among the brothers and then at the table. "Or Cosimo simply lied to your face to protect his ass."

"I think I know when I'm being lied to. I'm your Prez. Don't forget your place. You weren't there, VP. You'd have known."

"I wasn't there because you sent me to get intel from Alfarez."

"Did you?"

She pursed her lips. "Nothing useful as I anticipated. Which leads us back to square one. Wrench. Beth and he are planning to kill me and hijack our chapter, *Prez*. We must do something to stop them. Now."

"The last thing I want to do is put you in danger or let any threat whatsoever out there not taken care of, and I want to find Beth more than anyone, but something is fucking off."

"Why? Because of your Mob friend? It doesn't matter if he was the traitor or someone else was. Either way, the sabotage is over, and we're back on business. It has nothing to do with Beth. We need to find that woman yesterday."

"Claws have a point, Prez," Big Gun suddenly said. The other brothers agreed.

"Can you put my idea to a vote?" she asked.

I understood how she felt, having a target on her back. I did my best to make her feel safe, but after what happened to her and her sister by the hands of Roar, Beth and Rush, my own family, I didn't think there was anything I could do to convince her she didn't have to worry and I'd take care of her.

She needed the control. For her, I'd always been more than willing to give it to her. But not when it could destroy her.

"In the matter of raiding rivals in Detroit patches, what do you say? I'll vote first." I cocked a brow at her. "Nay."

She swore under her breath. "Well, yea."

"Yea," Skid followed. My Road Captain had become her fucking bitch. Ever since she saved his boy, whatever she said, he followed with a yea.

"Nay," Owl voted.

We all stared at Big Gun. He took his time as usual before he spoke. "Sorry, Prez. I'm with Claws on this one. Let's get our knives wet. Yea."

CHAPTER 40

DUSTY

I lost the next vote, too. If she had to go through with her plan, I needed to be with her on that raid, but it was a fucking unanimous vote that I shouldn't be there. They said if we found Beth, I could do something unpredictable that would compromise the raid, and Prez shouldn't get his hands dirty in the first place. The perks of being a fucking king in a democracy. I didn't get to protect my ol' fucking lady while she fought my battles. Battles that could be the end of us if Beth wasn't playing with Wrench.

Ginger came running through the clubhouse. "They're back."

I glanced at the monitor behind the bar. Our two SUVs were entering through the gate. I downed the last of my tequila shots and strode to the front yard.

The tires squealed on a brake, and Skid jumped off the driver's seat. "Ginger, get Owl. Prez, help me out."

I strode toward him. "What the fuck happened? Where is Cameron?"

"Claws is hurt."

My eyes widened as my feet flew toward the car. I almost dislocated the door to the backseat. Cammie's face was covered in blood, her good hand pressed on her bleeding shoulder, a t-shirt tied roughly around her calf.

"Don't give me that look. I'm all right," she said slowly, her eyes barely open.

I carried her in my arms and ran to the house, screaming, "Who the fuck did this?!"

Owl sprang from the door. "Put her on the kitchen counter."

One of the girls cleared the counter, pushing everything aside. I set Cammie down, my heart ringing in my ear. Her eyes were closing, and I started to panic. "Baby, baby, stay with me."

Owl removed her hand from her shoulder and swore. "Put your hand there. Keep pressure on it," he told me as he untied the t-shirt on her leg. He swore again. "I'm going to have to take the bullets out and stitch her up here. Hold her still while I get my bag and scrub my hands."

"Hurry up. She's gonna pass out."

"I need her to pass out."

Skid rushed inside. "How is she?"

"How the fuck did she get shot twice while you fuckers don't have a fucking scratch?!" I bellowed.

"Sorry, Prez. It's Beth. She was fast with the gun."

My heart skipped a beat. "Beth?"

He nodded. "Big Gun is taking her to the Boiler."

I glanced down at Cammie's face. A pale smile stretched on her lips "We got her."

Waves of emotions hit me all at once. They all contradicted each other. Victory. Anticipation. Relieve. Rage. Sadness. Guilt.

Heartbreak.

I kept waiting for this moment, but when it finally came, I realized I wasn't truly prepared for it.

CHAPTER 41

CAMERON

I coerced Owl to pump a shit load of painkillers in my veins after he patched me up. I wasn't going to wait till morning to pay that bitch my long-awaited visit.

Dusty begged me to rest. I ignored him, of course, and limbed out of the house. He accompanied me to the Boiler, every step an unspoken word.

"All this time she'd been with the Esqueletos Nomads," I said.

He took a deep breath and exhaled it. "Fuck."

"Yeah. Wrench had nothing to do with her. She was hiding under our noses like you said. You might be right about Cosimo, too. Esqueletos are a Mexican cartel club. They could be the ones who have been lacing the drugs." I wouldn't be surprised if Beth had been working with the Lanza traitor whoever he was to retaliate on Cosimo for backing Dusty when he wanted to leave. She betrayed Dusty and Roar before. It wouldn't have been hard for her to betray her friend as well. "But why? How did that aid her plan with Rush?"

"It's what we're about to know."

"Do you think she'll speak?"

"She will have no other choice," he grated.

I exhaled a long breath. "Are you mad at me?"

"To be honest…I am mad. Don't know if it's at you, though."

"You warned me, and I didn't listen. Now, Wrench is going to be pissed."

His eyes, the brightness vanishing into a demonic gloom, barely looked at me as the gravel and dirt crunched beneath our feet. "You still found her."

"And I promise, I know how to handle it here when all hell breaks loose…that is if you still trust me, of course."

He stopped and planted a kiss on my forehead. "That will never change."

He helped me down the stairs. Bending my leg wasn't a breeze. That bullet, unlike the one I got in the shoulder, almost got to the bone. When we arrived at the Boiler door, he reached for the handlebar. I grabbed his hand in a flash. "I'll take it from here."

"I'm going in there," he stated.

"To say goodbye?"

His jaws clenched. His eyes became fatal. "She shot at you."

"She's done way worse. Now, I'll make her pay," I said coldly. I wasn't angry or emotional or even victorious, my brick wall a shield I wouldn't give up yet. I was on a mission. A task I needed done. "Go back to the house and wait for my return."

"I'm going in there," he spat.

"You can't touch her."

"I won't," he lied. I felt it.

"She'd beg you to save her," I warned.

"Then I'll shut her up for good. I'm going in there, Cammie. There's nothing you're going to say or do to stop me."

Shaking my head, I threw my hands in the air in surrender. "Fine."

He pushed the handlebar and opened the door. Big Gun was standing inside, blocking the view. He moved away when we entered.

Gagged, bound and coiled up in a corner, Beth mumbled incoherent pleas through her tears. The menacing heat coming from Dusty's body as he saw her thrashed my heart. He stalked toward her, fire shooting out of his stare.

"That's far enough, Prez," Big Gun said.

Dusty hushed him with one stare. Then he made him leave the room. Big Gun obeyed without a word. When he shut the door behind us, Dusty crouched down before the bitch and ripped the duct tape off her mouth in one swift move. She cried out in pain, and begged for her son's mercy, her limbs writhing and kicking at the ropes.

He stared at her for minutes before he finally said, "You took away everything that mattered to me."

"No, sweetheart. I'm your Mama. I love you. I'd never hurt you."

"Shut the fuck up."

"No, you gotta believe me. I only worked with the Italians because they'd have never touched you. They wanted you here, too. It was my only condition."

He narrowed his gaze at her. "You and Rush went behind my back and Cosimo's and betrayed the MC, our family and our friends, why?"

"I wanted you to stay President. I didn't want you to leave." She shot daggers at me with her hateful stare. "She had to get out of your way. Rush was scared you'd kill him like Roar if he hurt her so he made an arrangement with the Lanzas. I was supposed to go there while they pretended they took me and then they'd demand you stay Prez to protect their business or they'd kill me if you refused or killed Rush."

"What made them so sure I'd save you or him after what you'd done?"

He face paled, and her lips quivered.

"It wasn't just in exchange for your safety and your fucking dog's life, was it? They'd have killed me if I chose not to be a pawn in their filthy game."

A sudden blast of anger ran through me. How much she hated me and how far she was willing to go to get rid of me was palpable, but to make a deal with the Mafia against her own son—my boyfriend—that would threaten his own life? That was a new level of low that I couldn't begin to fathom, even now when I'd become one with this shithole.

She shook her head rapidly, her eyes wide. "I'd have never let them hurt you. It was all fake just until you knew you belonged here and gave up on her. Cosimo had to pay for what he'd done, too. He was helping you leave. He betrayed me first."

"The things I'm gonna do to that heart of yours before you take your last breath…" I murmured, picturing it already.

She spat in my face and swore.

My fist clenched, but Dusty blocked her out of my sight and grabbed her hair, pulling her neck back so far she whimpered. "You made that deal with the Lanzas in exchange for what?"

"Just working with the Esqueletos to lace the crack. It was one of many hits they'd already arranged. They wanted Cosimo out, and they'd pin all the deals that had been going wrong for them on him." She cried. "But when they got rid of Cosimo, they stopped their protection. They sold me the fuck out. Without Rush or you, without the brothers I was as good as dead. I'm glad you found me. You're my baby. You wouldn't kill me, Dusty. I'm your mother. I love you. I love you so much."

"You sent my father to rape my ol'lady. You betrayed me and the MC. You killed my unborn child."

"I didn't know she was pregnant. I'm so sorry, sweetheart. I did everything I could to give you the best life you can ever have. I'm so sorry."

He pursed his lips, staring at her for long unreadable moments as she begged and blubbered. Would he forgive her? Did he still find it in his heart to spare that bitch?

I wouldn't let it happen. He couldn't do this to me.

I was about to open my mouth and protest, ready to kick him out of the Boiler if I had to. No one was going to stop me from having my revenge on the woman that destroyed my life.

He slapped his thighs and rose to his feet. "I'm sorry, too."

"No, no! Dusty, please. I'm your mother! Don't let her do this to me!"

"Who betrayed Cosimo, Beth? Was it Enzio? He went that far because he wanted the throne?" he asked, but who cared about the Lanzas?

She looked up at him, suddenly calm. "I'll tell you, but you have to let me go. You need this info to know who you're dealing with and who to trust."

That bitch. Bargaining for her life until the very end. "We don't give a shit. We'll find out on our own. You're not leaving the Boiler alive so save your breath for when I work on you."

Realization hit her face. Horror stroke her eyes, and I smirked. "Dusty! *Dusty!* Don't let her kill me! DUSTY! I'm your mother. You can't do this to me." She blubbered ugly at the end.

"A mother wouldn't hold info about motherfuckers who could end up killing him to bargain with for her pathetic, cheating, backstabbing life. My mother wouldn't kill my baby before it had a chance to live."

The anger I felt out of my protectiveness of Dusty earlier turned into flames at the reminder of the life she took from me. Then came the stabs in my heart that would never stop. I closed my eyes, searching for that wall that was falling apart around my heart. *Not tonight. Not until it was all done.*

Dusty opened the door and nodded at Big Gun to come back in. Then Dusty marched my way. When he reached me, he didn't look at me, but he said, "Make her scream. And enjoy it."

The door slammed shut, the bang louder than it should have been. The pain in both my shoulder and calf was waking up, but it was nothing compared to the aches waking in my heart. It wasn't going to stop me from finishing what I came here to do, though.

Nothing would.

I eyed the tools on the bench, and then glanced at the bitch. The agonized, fearful look in her eyes made the pain throbbing through me worth every second.

"I will, Prez."

CHAPTER 42

CAMERON

I went into the Boiler cold and numb, as I'd been for weeks. I came out with more blood on my hands and more cold darkness in my soul.

I had to smother the emotions that fought through the surface and threatened to ruin my plans. I did enjoy every scream, every blood drop, every plea, though. Torturing that miserable cunt made me horny as fuck. It beat me why I was surprised and not very pleased with my nature right now. Torturing Dusty at the bunker had the same effect. Maybe I'd convinced myself it made sense with him because he was a man and hot as sin. But I'd always known there was more to it.

Just like that day I'd discovered my kinky side in bed, today I discovered I was a true sadist, not just a dominant woman in the sheets.

I was a sadist killer who got her rocks off on her victims' pain. I'd become someone way worse than the Dusty I rejected for beating an asshole like Samuel. Someone like the fucker I shot and the lowlife I'd just tortured to death for revenge.

Did I like that person I'd become? I didn't think so. Did I care?

Fuck no.

As if a humanity switch was real, in the Boiler, before the feelings I'd been bottling down consumed me, I had to turn that switch off entirely. The question was, could it be turned back on or had I lost myself and my soul forever and turned into that monster I'd always feared and loathed to be come?

My mind didn't even try to justify what I'd done. I didn't need to tell myself they hurt me and what I did was justice. Even my inner voice was silent. As if getting hurt entitled me to hurt back unapologetically, without an ounce of regret or guilt.

Dusty was right after all. This place sucked your soul dry until there was nothing left.

Big Gun helped me back to the house. Then I washed off the blood before I headed to the bedroom. I knew Dusty was there, waiting for me to come back. I didn't want him to see his mother's blood on my hands.

The second I entered the room, I saw the strangest expression on his face. He had a huge grin on his mouth as tears streamed down his cheeks.

I took off all my clothes, and he held my naked body close to his. His eyes still brought the memories, but they didn't torment me anymore.

His heated breath teased my lips. "Is it over?"

I tangled my hands in his hair and pressed my mouth to his. "Yes."

He pulled away, his lips swollen. His glistening gaze bore into mine, as if searching for a different answer. "No, it isn't."

Before I asked him what he meant, he tugged at the end of his t-shirt and slid it over his head.

CHAPTER 43

DUSTY

She didn't use the blindfold.

I should have been happy, over the fucking moon for feeling her sweet pussy tightening around my cock over and over after weeks of blue balls. For seeing her beautiful eyes glaze over and roll back as I sent her moaning and purring my name.

But I was numb, too. I'd say I was sheltering myself from the pain of losing my mother, the same way Cammie had been doing since Ash. But no. I'd stopped caring about Beth the second I knew about my baby. I was numb because Cameron rubbed off on me pretty bad. The only person who had made me feel something different other than the shit in my world now was the reason I was back in this dump, feeling nothing but it. Especially with that vacant look in her eyes. The look I'd seen on many faces around here.

I was numb because I didn't want to feel the pain that came with losing my Cammie to Claws.

I thought when Beth was gone, Cammie would stop being that empty shell, would come back to me. But last night I knew my Cammie was gone for good. There was only Claws.

The only time she looked like her old self was when she was spending time with Carter. I once made the mistake of telling her she'd have made a great mother. She stopped talking to the boy completely after.

I sank down into a chair at the kitchen table. The sweetbutts set me with my coffee and some eggs along with the glorious view of their tits almost falling out of their tops.

People were dancing, smoking weed, and slamming shots in the middle of the day. One couple was off in the corner, having sex against the wall. Owl, Ginger, Chain and Serial blocked the sun one by one as they entered the house.

Owl filled himself a cup of coffee. "Morning, Prez."

"What's up?"

He found a chair. "Stacking arms for the big fun."

"Found anything on Wrench?"

"The birds are everywhere. We'll see who sings. We're ready for him and his pack of dogs any time anyway."

There was a new brunette on the other side of the kitchen counter where I sat. College age. Curvy, wearing a yellow bikini. I missed Cammie's all brown hair. She'd bleached parts of it blonde without even asking me and got so many fucking tattoos I stopped counting. None of them were skulls or roses, though. Maybe, it was a good sign there was still hope she didn't truly want to stay here. "You filled the pool last night or something?"

Owl cackled. "Nah. It's Ginger that picked her up from a pool party."

"Ginger?" I ruffled the boy's head as he passed right by me. "Way to go, kid. Older women are hot in the sheets." Cammie was a couple of years older and that alone stirred my cock in my pants.

He winked at me.

I rolled my eyes at Owl. "Did the fucker just wink at me?"

The doctor dipped his nose in his steamy cup. "I think he did."

A chuckle escaped me. I'd go after Ginger, but I didn't want to make him look bad in front of his bitch.

He said something in her ear, and she glanced over at me, flashing a smile. In a second, she was next to me, tits pressed against my shoulder and her hand resting on my thigh. I was about to tell her to move along, when Cammie came down the stairs.

Shit.

"This will be fun," Owl said.

I pushed the chair back, my hand reaching to push the girl aside. But something told me to wait and see what Cammie would do first.

To see jealousy in my woman's eyes instead of the blankness. To watch her in a catfight. To know there was still emotions down there. Any kind. It really could be fun and…heartwarming.

Cameron glanced at the couple fucking against the wall and rolled her eyes back on me and Owl. "Huh? The party started early today." With a fucking smile on her face, she went over to the coffee pot and poured herself a cup. Then she headed to the fridge, got ice-cream out of the freezer, grabbed a spoon and put a little scoop in the coffee.

"I'll suck you until you blow your load down my throat, and then I'll suck you some more," the girl in the bikini said, low enough to be sexy, loud enough for Cameron to hear.

My own fucking ol'lady kept mixing ice-cream with coffee, blind and deaf. A whore was offering to suck her ol'man's cock right under her nose, and she was being a fucking cold bitch.

Cameron suppressed a yawn before her boots echoed outside of the kitchen. "I have to be at the Little Wicked all day today, but you know how to reach me."

The room shrank in silence. It was as if everybody was holding their breaths, waiting for big action, and the show was cancelled last minute.

Cameron didn't push between me and the bitch. She didn't grab her, pull her hair, throw her backwards or break any of her bones. Not even a threat or a *fuck you*.

"That's it?" Owl was the first to speak.

I jutted upward and smashed my cup against the wall. The hot liquid splattered all over, generating a few yelps from the rest of the bitches. "Yeah, that's it. What the fuck did you expect?"

I twisted, grabbed the bikini bitch's shaking hand and put it on my flat dick. "You're new, but they should've told you Prez has nothing for you here." The second I let her hand go, she ran away.

My stare traveled around every face in the room. "That's how solid Claws and Dusty are. She knows it. I know it. It's time all of you knew it, too."

A few grunts hummed as I stalked to the stairs. They surely didn't buy my lies, but who the fuck cared? I asked myself one question, the one that mattered, my heart a million pieces.

How long would I be lying to myself before I knew Cameron wasn't in love with me anymore?

CHAPTER 44

CAMERON

I hurt him again.

He must have thought I didn't care about some bitch in a fucking bikini touching him and offering to suck his dick. He must have thought I'd become too cold to be even jealous.

But there were many things Dusty didn't know.

He didn't know I still loved him no matter how hard I tried not to. He didn't know how much power he had over me that he was my only weakness now. He didn't know that since I'd felt him inside me again, the brick wall was, despite my efforts, dissolving, one brick after another. He wasn't aware that I'd been slipping out of bed early in the morning every day to watch Skid driving Carter off to school through the window without him seeing me. And today, I knew Skid was taking him back to his mother, and I just couldn't bring myself to come down and say goodbye.

He couldn't tell that all the time I'd been making my coffee, I was seriously thinking about burning the brunette's face on the fucking stove.

Why hadn't I showed him any of this?

Because I had to hold on to what was left of my brick wall for a little longer. If I broke down now, everything I'd worked so hard for, everything I'd paid for in blood, would be lost.

Beth wasn't the end of my revenge. It was only the beginning.

Just a few more nights, Dusty. Just a few more nights, my love.

CHAPTER 45

DUSTY

"Meet me at the Little Wicked @ 9."

I woke up to that text from Cameron. Squinting at my side, I saw she wasn't there. I looked at the clock on my phone. 11 a.m. Fuck. I barely saw her last night, and now she was already out that early and planning to stay at the titty bar all day.

Ok. We gotta talk. I texted back.

Tonight was the night I sorted shit out. No more lies. No more secrets. The end of this charade.

At seven, I met Skid at the gates. He was coming back with his kid. "What the hell?"

"Just till tonight, Prez. That bi…" He clawed is hands at the air, swallowing the curse so Carter wouldn't hear it.

I shook my head, but one look at the boy's eyes tugged at my heart. "Get inside, but you gotta move him in the morning. It's not safe here."

"I know. I'll send him over to my sister till it's done, but she has a shift tonight and can't have him."

I got on my bike and roared off the gates. I had something important to do before meeting Cameron.

Music streamed from the club as I turned off the engine and walked inside. Purple and yellow lights dimmed my vision. Bouncing tits and pole dances greeted me as I cruised through the grating bodies. I reached the bar. Serena and Candy were making out topless on top of the bar for extra tips from the thirsty, cheering crowd.

I waited the show over before I tapped on the counter. Serena came running to me with a shaking smile. "Get you anything, Dusty?"

"Claws?"

She pressed away that smile as I felt arms wrapping around my shoulders. I turned, and Cameron was there. She pulled me in for a long, hot kiss, pushing her hips against mine. "Right here."

I grabbed on my anger to shield me from what her kiss was still capable of doing to me. "We need to talk."

"I know." She smiled, leading me to the dance floor. "Dance with me first."

"Not in the mood. And your leg is hurt."

"Please."

I sighed and moved with her. For a moment or two, I was lost in the way her hips swayed against my cock. But the heartache she'd left me with all alone for days every day since she woke up wouldn't let me forget.

My hands dropped off her waist. "We gotta talk, Cameron. Now."

She pulled me in for another kiss, and then bit my earlobe. "We will once we get out of here. Just play along."

Play along? I laughed at myself. All the kissing and touching and dancing was another act to get whatever the fuck she wanted now. I leaned in close to her ear. "I'm done with your shit…Claws."

That dark side of hers didn't speak to me anymore. It'd fucked up everything.

Drawing back, I almost forced her off me when she used all her strength to keep me in her embrace. She stretched on her toes and bent my head to her shoulder. "I swear it's nothing like that. But Serena needs to see that we're good and ready to fuck all night at home. So please just play along," she whispered.

I pretended to kiss her neck. "Is she…"

"Yes. I'll tell you everything when we leave." She met my eyes, and for the first time in weeks, her smile touched her gaze. "Trust me?"

"With my life."

"Love me?"

What the fuck were you doing to me, Cammie? Asking me that question, melting my heart with two words just like that? I brushed my thumb over her cheek, holding her face with my hand and let out the most heated sigh I'd ever breathed. "Always. Do you?"

She smiled. "Ask me that question at the end of the night."

CHAPTER 46

CAMERON

Wrapping my arms around my man's waist, feeling his warm body pressed against mine, smelling his musk as we rode through the night brought back beautiful memories of peaceful times.

Tonight was my last chance to put everything behind me and find peace again.

I didn't answer any of Dusty's questions until we returned to Rosewood. We made a quick appearance to make sure everybody saw us, and then I led him to the Boiler.

"You found out the blonde bitch is Wrench's spy and you're dragging me down here right now? We gotta alert the brothers. Wrench can be barging into Rosewood any minute," he said.

"He will be here in less than five minutes," she whispered. "I heard the bitch arranging the raid with him on the phone myself."

"What? And you tell me now?" He blamed me with his eyes, letting go of my hand.

"Listen to me." I held on to his slipping fingers. "We'll take the back exit from here and into the woods. I already hid my bike there. We'll leave and never look back like we were supposed to," I panted nervously.

The temptation in his eyes was evident but so was the torment. "I can't leave my brothers under fire." He yanked his hand out of mine and spun back.

"No, Dusty. You can't go back in there."

"Just wait for me in the woods. I'll come find you when it's over."

"No... The whole place will blow up!"

He stopped in his tracks and slowly turned to me. "What did you do?"

"What I needed to do. It's the only way to move on."

His tight grip squeezed my arms, shaking me hard. "That was your fucking plan all along? What the fuck did you do?"

"What I had to do so it'd finally be over!" My heart ached in flames. "I'd tried to walk away. I'd tried to let you run things differently without getting involved. And when both failed, I'd tried to wait for you until you were out so we could start fucking living, but look what happened? I lost everything to this place. Annie, Ash, our baby, my future, my fucking soul, *everything*."

"There are people up there. They trusted you with their lives as much as I did. They ate with you, fought with you, protected your ass as much as they could," he roared.

"And it's gonna shatter my already broken heart later when we're miles away from here. But we both know there are no innocents up there. They didn't bat an eye when Roar kidnapped a fifteen-year-old to abuse and murder just because he could. They watched Beth and Rush hurt me I almost lost my life while innocents like Ashley, like our unborn child, were brutally killed in the aftermath, and what did they do?"

"Cameron—"

"The Night Skulls has to be destroyed. Along with Wrench and his Skulls and everything threatening our fucking lives. It's the only way, and you know it."

His bitter eyes widened at me while his jaws clenched. "Carter is up there."

"What?" I shook my head hysterically. "He left yesterday. I saw him go with Skid with my own eyes."

"He brought him back a few hours ago."

The last brick in the wall had fallen to the ground. My head spun. All the pain I'd been storing, hiding, suffocating gnawed at my flesh and my soul.

Several muffled bangs seeped through the ceiling. Gunshots. Wrench must have arrived.

Dusty looked up and around him. Then he shook me again. "Whatever the fuck you did, stop it now."

Dazed, I just stared back at him. "I can't. I was afraid I'd back down so I already set it to blow up while we were out."

"When?"

"Nine minutes from now."

"Fuck!"

We flew out of the back exit only to buy more time away from the shooting range. For a better chance to get Carter out of here.

The odds didn't look good, though. By the number of bullets flaring right and left, I'd say the chances for anyone to get out of here were slim to none. In this instant, however, I didn't care about my life. Only Carter's. And Dusty's.

As I limped to the backside of the house, Dusty, his gun out, covered my back. Once we got inside, I saw Owl dragging his bleeding leg behind the bar, a rifle in his hand. Big Gun was stabbing someone to death, Skid, a big gash on his forehead, slitting another guy's throat with his dagger.

"Just get Carter," Dusty mouthed as he pushed me up the stairs. Before I could object, he entered the kitchen and started shooting.

I ran up to the upper floor where the brothers' rooms were, not minding the searing pain in my leg. Thank God Wrench's Skulls hadn't reached that part of the house. Yet.

Dashing to Skid's room, I felt warm liquid on my calf. Great. I fucked up my stitches. I pushed the door open as quietly as possible. Carter was huddled in a corner in bunny pajamas, headphones covering his ears.

I placed my index finger on my mouth to tell him to stay quiet. He obliged and let me carry him out of the room. He shook in my arms as I raced against time to get him out of Rosewood.

Guns banged in the background as I reached the area behind the Boiler. I put

Carter down, squatted to his level and lifted off his headphones. "Listen to me, champ. You see those woods?" I pointed to the left.

He nodded.

"I need you to run there as fast as you can and never stop for anything until you see a shiny Harley under a big tree. Can you do that for me, champ?"

He nodded again. "Are you gonna be there?"

"Yes. Yes, champ. Just like the last time. You can always count on me to be there."

"Okay, Cameron." He gave me a tiny hug that sent tears welling up in my eyes. "I love you."

I couldn't hold my tears back. "I love you too, buddy. Now run."

He sprinted to the woods. I waited until he vanished in the dark, and then I darted back to the house.

It didn't matter that the bombs I set inside every building in Rosewood would blow in a couple of minutes. It didn't matter I was going to die. The only thing that mattered was Dusty. I had to get him out of here even if I had to drag him out myself.

I wouldn't let the only man I'd ever loved die for my mistakes, even if my life was the price.

CHAPTER 47

CAMERON

The kitchen was a battlefield. Our Skulls were shooting and gutting anyone who came close to the inside of the house. To them, this was the last fortress. If it fell, Wrench's Skulls would win.

Nobody but Dusty and I knew there were no winners tonight.

Blood and smoke filled the air making it too hard to see clearly. I couldn't find Dusty, so I ducked, grabbing the first gun I saw on the floor. It was still in the bloody grip of one of the dead bodies there.

Checking the bullets, I rolled behind a counter and found Skid. His body was jerking on the floor, a big hole in his chest. He opened his mouth, blood trickling down of it. "Carter," he rattled.

"Safe. Dusty?" I whispered, closing his wound with my palm, a man's head looming on the other side of the counter.

"Couch."

Bang. Bang!

The head hit the counter and then disappeared.

"Go," Skid rattled again.

"I'm sorry," I mouthed. Then I rolled, zigzagged among the bodies and ducked behind the couch.

Dusty's eyes widened at me. His index finger pointed sharply at the kitchen backdoor.

I shook my head, noticing Big Gun's bald head behind the facing couch. "We gotta move," I mouthed at Dusty, telling him with my fingers I had one bullet in my gun.

"Fuck," he said under his breath as Big Gun jumped to our side. He gestured with his piece for us to go.

More men rumbled through the door. They were ours. Their gunshots flashed as one of them boomed, "Save Prez."

Dusty took my hand and dragged me the same way I got in. Just as we reached a point a couple of feet across from the front door, the men barricading it fell dead. Then five of Wrench's Skulls and their Prez himself barged in.

Exposed, Dusty shielded me with his body. "Run."

Big Gun jumped over the couch, tackling two of the men. The surprise startled them, and they started shooting in every direction. Dusty, still shielding me, aimed successfully at two other men, sending them to their hell. I shot the last of Wrench's men with my only bullet.

Dusty had nothing between him and Wrench except for the piled bodies on the floor. Dusty squeezed his trigger only to find out at the worst time ever he, too, was out of bullets.

He pushed me back to give me a head start. "Fucking run!"

I dragged Dusty by the hand, urging him to run with me. Adrenalin pumped in my veins, letting the blood from my wound stream faster. It countered the waves of nausea I had from bleeding and delayed my inevitable unconsciousness and bleeding out.

"Go with her!" Big Gun's bellowing scream
clogged in his throat as Wrench put a bullet in
his head. Then the gun was pointed at Dusty
and me.

"No one is going anywhere. You two are
coming with me where I make a fucking
example out of you," Wrench snarled, taking a
step toward us. I took in his ugly, old face. He
had a scar across the left side of his cheek,
another under his right eye, missing teeth and
a heavy beard. His eyes steel blue. His gray
hair long and greasy.

This whole place was gonna blow up in less
than a minute. The first bomb to start was
right in this fucking house. I had to do
something. Anything. My eyes darted around,
landing on a kitchen knife on the bar.

"Not gonna happen, fucker." Dusty
swooped down on Wrench, sending him flat
on his ass on the porch. I grabbed the knife
and bolted to the door. Wrench still had the
gun in his hand, and just as Dusty was lunging
at him again...

Bang.

"Dusty!" Terror shot through me as smoke
trickled from Wrench's gun and Dusty's
President patch turned red.

Wrench gave me a sickening grin as he
pointed his piece at me. My eyes yawed

between him and Dusty's bleeding body on the porch.

The last piece of my sanity shattered. I kicked the gun off Wrench's hand without bothering if it'd go off in my face. Then, screaming wildly, I burst and pinned the motherfucker down with my weight even though he was double my size. With all my force, I swung back the blade in my fists and stabbed the son of a bitch straight in the heart. Countless times.

Something grabbed at my foot, snapping me out of my spree. It took me a moment to register it was Dusty's hand.

"The bomb," I reminded myself in horror. Dropping the knife, I got off Wrench and dragged Dusty by the wrists down the porch steps...

Boom.

I swirled in the air, my arms flailing, heat searing my back. Then I hit the ground smashing my ribs.

Pain throbbed through every cell of my body, but I was glad I didn't pass out. I tried to get up, immediately falling on my ass. "Dusty!" I yelled in succession, dragging myself around in the smoke.

The clubhouse burst in flames before my eyes, and I screamed at the top of my lungs, watching what I had done with my own hands.

My big fucking plan.

I had my revenge. I razed Rosewood to the ground. I killed them all. Every last one of the Night Skulls. The good and the bad. Even the one guy that sacrificed his own life for me. I killed Dusty.

"Ahhhh," I wailed in unbearable pain, crying my eyes out. "Dusty!" My body gave and coiled up on the blazing ground, ready to fucking go to the hell I deserved.

CHAPTER 48

CAMERON

"Princess!"

Owl. He was alive?

"Princess!"

No. My head spun with hallucinations as I bled out.

"Princess! I got him!"

Life sprang through me against all odds. I pushed myself up, grunting in pain, hoping beyond hope it was real. "Owl? Is that you?"

"I got him. Let's get you out of here." The smoke thinned, and I could see Owl, holding Dusty's unconscious body under his shoulder, dragging him and himself toward me.

"Oh my God. Dusty!" I wiped my eyes fast. "Is he breathing?"

"Yes. We gotta get out of here."

My heart fluttered as my mind worked fast. "The SUV. You gotta make a run for it before the parking lot explodes, too."

"And you?" Owl asked, already started to the parking lot.

"I'll get Carter and find you. I have my bike."

In the next hour or so, I felt as if I was out of my body. I had no recollection how I reached Carter or rode down the road with him. But I did.

We ended up at the clinic of Vet, our backup doctor—he was literally a vet but he knew his way around stitches and bullets—and Owl's bunk-mate when they were in the military, right outside the borders of Sacramento. Vet closed his clinic and patched the three of us as best as he could, while Carter waited with the one sick puppy in the clinic.

Owl and I weren't as badly hurt as Dusty. He was the one in danger. I waited by his bed, monitoring his breathing and heart rhythm as if my life depended on them.

It did.

Without Dusty, I had no reason to survive. I wouldn't be able to get over what I'd done.

I held his hand and cried through the night, letting all my regressed feelings out. I prayed and begged him to wake up. I told him how sorry I was and how much I wished I'd told him that I loved him when he asked. Now, I might have no chance to make him hear it again.

I spent the rest of one of the longest nights of my life in silence and anticipation. The early rays of dawn shone through the shutters of the clinic's windows and danced on Dusty's face. I planted a little kiss on the back of his hand and his forehead. "I love you, Dusty. More than you'll ever know."

Tears stained my face again. "You gotta live, baby. For me. For everything we've ever dreamed of. For our life together. For the family we'll start and all the babies we'll make." I bent my forehead to his hand and pressed it. "Please, Dusty. I need you. You can't leave me. I know you gave up on me, and you wanted to break things off when you came to the strip club. After what I've done, you wouldn't want to see my face ever again, but I can't live without you. Please."

"How many?"

My head snapped up at the slur, and the bright green eyes glittered at me. "Dusty," I rasped, squeezing gently at his hand.

"How many babies?"

I laughed through the tears. "As many as you want."

"Promise?"

"Yes." I giggled, kissing his palm. "Yes, Dusty. There's something I haven't told you. That night when we broke up and you were so adamant about putting a baby in me, I'd told myself I forgot to take the morning after pill, but I didn't forget. I didn't take it on purpose. It was as if I wanted to stay tied to you even after we broke up. Despite everything, I was so happy when I found out I was late. I wanted our baby so much, Dusty."

Faintly, his fingers twitched around mine, and tears sparkled in his gaze. "I didn't give up on you. I have a confession to make, too. Before I came to you, I went to Enzio."

"What? Why? He could have killed you after what Beth did."

"I was telling him we were leaving whether he liked it or not."

"We?"

"You and me. I was going to kidnap you, if I had to, and take you so far away from Rosewood. I couldn't just watch you lose another piece of your soul until there was nothing left."

My heart squeezed. "You didn't give up on me. You wanted to save me."

"If only I did it a day earlier..."

I moaned a sigh that felt like a blunt blade in my chest. "I'm so sorry, baby."

"Carter?"

"Outside with Owl."

"Anyone else?"

Skid and Big Gun's faces as they sacrificed their lives for us would forever haunt me. I shook my head, wishing I'd been dead instead of them.

Dusty's eyes squeezed shut. His breath labored as he inhaled.

"Please forgive me, Dusty. I know I don't deserve it, just like the brothers I killed didn't deserve to die either. They gave their lives to protect us, without knowing I was the reason they were dead. Carter trusted me, not knowing he lost his father and uncle because of me."

His eyes reddened with tears. "The first time you call them brothers..."

"I can say I'm sorry for the rest of my life, but it'd never be enough. I'm ready for whatever punishment you see fit. Anything you'd do to me would be mercy compared to living with what I'd done. I just need you to know I never meant to hurt you. You're all that matters to me in this world."

Weakly, he lifted my hand to his mouth and kissed my fingertips. "It was inevitable. We all make mistakes, Cammie, and you were hurting. I love you, and I forgive you. But I need to know if you feel the same way about me."

I went closer and brushed his hair off his forehead. Then I kissed him as softly as I could. "I do."

"Love me?" he asked.

I smiled through the tears. "Forever."

EPILOGUE
DOWNLOAD IT HERE

https://bookhip.com/PTHWBGT

Thanks for Reading and Playlist!

I hope you enjoyed the final part of Dusty and Cameron's story as much as I enjoyed writing it. I cried my eyes out during several moments in this series!

Read Furore and Tirone duet in the same series
https://books2read.com/furore
and the series sequel Night Skulls Mayhem
https://books2read.com/NightSkullsM

If you haven't read Forbidden Cruel Italians Mafia series and anxious to know who the Lanzas are, this is for you:
- **Start The Italians series PREQUEL FREE with The Cruel Italian**
https://BookHip.com/RCSXCGR
For Enzio Lanza's book, read and download The Italian Marriage now

Join my Newsletter for extra scenes, free
books and updates
Njadelbooks.com

SOUNDTRACK

Listen to the full playlist on Spotify
https://spoti.fi/3SUaW0Z

ALSO BY N.J. ADEL

Contemporary Romance
The Italian Heartthrob
The Italian Happy Ever After
The Italian Marriage
The Italian Obsession
The Italian Dom
The Italian Son

Paranormal Reverse Harem
All the Teacher's Pet Beasts
All the Teacher's Little Belles
All the Teacher's Bad Boys
All the Teacher's Prisoners

Reverse Harem Erotic Romance
Her Royal Harem: Complete Box Set

Dark MC and Mafia Romance
Furore
Tirone
Dusty
Cameron
Night Skulls Mayhem

AUTHOR BIO

N. J. Adel, the author of All the Teacher's Pets, Her Royal Harem, The Italians, and The Night Skulls MC series, is a cross genre author. From chocolate to books and book boyfriends, she likes it DARK and SPICY.

Bikers, rock stars, dirty Hollywood heartthrobs, smexy guards and men who serve. She loves it all.

She is a loather of cats and thinks they are Satan's pets. She used to teach English by day and write fun smut by night with her German Shepherd, Leo. Now, she only writes the fun smut.

Printed in Great Britain
by Amazon